I0676145

A Certain Slant of Light

Dale T. Phillips

Try these other works by Dale T. Phillips

Shadow of the Wendigo (Supernatural Thriller)

The Zack Taylor Mystery Series
A Memory of Grief
A Fall From Grace
A Shadow on the Wall

Story Collections
Fables and Fantasies (Fantasy)
Crooked Paths (Mystery/Crime)
More Crooked Paths (Mystery/Crime)
Strange Tales (Magic Realism, Paranormal)
Apocalypse Tango (Science Fiction)
Halls of Horror (Horror)
Jumble Sale (Mixed Genres)
The Big Book of Genre Stories (Different Genres)

DEDICATION

Life is a perilous, lonely journey, and writing is our attempt to deal with it. Many thanks to the wonderful people who have helped me and stood by me, even in the difficult times

ACKNOWLEDGMENTS

Zack is back. At long last– a number of people have been asking for his next adventure, and here it is. It took even longer than expected, because of life getting ever-more difficult. There were extensive revision tasks to do– the results of a great editing staff, who were able to diligently improve the action and text. A hearty thank you to Ursula Wong, Ray Daniel, Vlad Vaslyn, Stacey Longo, and Rob Smales– all authors in their own right, but who took the time and effort to read this work (some multiple times) and offer their suggestions to make it better.

My thanks extend to everyone who helped to make this book possible.

To writer Dana King, who understands the world of Zack Taylor deeply, and who allowed me to use his kind and generous words of praise. (His novels are great– buy them– starting with the Penns River books!)

As always, to my wonderful family: Mindy, Bridget, and Erin, for suffering my solitary profession of writing.

To my dear and supportive friends and loved ones for making things more enjoyable along the path of life.

To all those who have helped teach me to write, through their works.

To all those who read other Zack Taylor mysteries and wanted more.

And to you, dear reader, my thanks, for reading this one.

Feel free to contact me and let me know what you thought of the book and what it's about.

A Certain Slant of Light

There's a certain Slant of light,

Winter Afternoons –

That oppresses, like the Heft

Of Cathedral Tunes –

When it comes, the Landscape listens –

Shadows – hold their breath –

When it goes, 'tis like the Distance

On the look of Death –

—Emily Dickinson

CHAPTER 1

A deathbed request is one you don't refuse. So I didn't, though I hated being asked. I'd flown from Maine down here to Miami because she'd asked me to. *She* being Marguerite "Rita" Harris, my former landlady who'd become my friend.

As I made my way through the hospital corridors, I heard the squeak of the nurses' shoes as they made their rounds, and smelled the cleaning fluids that tried to mask the odors that came with sickness and death. I hated being in a hospital again, as people I'd loved had died in places like this sterile tomb. And I'd been forced to spend too much time in hospitals recovering from the effects of my stupidity and poor choices. Being here brought back some bad memories.

Sunshine streamed through the window of her room, illuminating the dying woman in the bed, and enveloping her in a halo of white light. I hesitated at the door, not seeing any movement of her frail form. If she was sleeping, I didn't want to wake her.

I edged silently closer. Only the slightest rise and fall of her chest indicated she was still breathing. The ravages of cancer had left little resemblance to the strong, vibrant woman I'd said goodbye to just the year before. Swallowing, I couldn't get rid of the lump in my throat.

There was a book on the stand by her bed, a collection of poetry by Emily Dickinson. The Belle of Amherst had written about visitations from Death, and here was a woman who would soon meet him. I opened to where the bookmark lay, and read, my voice low.

"*There's a certain slant of light*," I said, but couldn't finish.

Her eyelids fluttered open, and she gave me a weak smile. "Zack." Her voice was like the rustle of dry paper. She looked as if she'd been squeezed like an orange, all of life's juices gone. Tubes snaked from her in different directions, modern medicine keeping her in this world. It didn't seem like a mercy.

I gently touched the tips of her fingers. "Hey there."

She reached to grip my hand as if afraid I'd run away. "Must ask you for a promise."

I knew I wasn't going to like what she was about to ask. "What?"

"Find my grandson, Steven. I need to see him."

"You've lost touch?"

"Some time back, he came to see me. He hadn't been by for a while. He wanted the Dali you like that's hanging in my living room. It's genuine. Worth a bit."

"And you said no."

"He'd have just sold it. He said he had to have money, or he'd be forced to do something bad."

"Like what?"

"He told me he could make good money copying paintings that were sold as genuine. He thought I'd weaken."

I smiled. "Didn't work very well, did it?"

"I gave him some money, but wouldn't give him the Dali. He was angry. I haven't heard from him since."

"Any idea where he is?"

"Card in the drawer." She made a faint gesture to the stand beside the bed. Throughout the conversation, she'd seemed to fade in and out, like a distant radio station.

I opened the drawer and took out a business card. "Saul Rabinowitz, Attorney at Law." I looked at her. "He's the one who contacted me. Good Irish name."

She gave me a weak smile. "He'll explain everything."

"What do I do when I find Steven?"

"Bring him here. He'll come, since there's some money from my estate. Late, but better than never."

"Does he get the Dali, now, too?"

"No. It's for you."

"Me?"

"You always loved it. You'll take care of it, protect it. Not just sell it off for cash. It has great sentimental value."

"You met him, didn't you?"

"Salvador? Oh, yes. He was something, I can tell you that. A true artist, but such a joker. It was after the war, when people were getting back into life and art. A fun crowd back then. Quite an experience." She had a faraway look, remembering places of long ago. "I had so many interesting experiences. Now, nobody will know or care."

"I care," I said. "I can stay here, and you can tell me about them."

"No. You have to find Steven. I need to see him before I go. Promise me you'll bring him back in time."

I hesitated. I didn't want to say I could do something that I might not be able to make happen. What if I couldn't find him in time? What if he didn't want to come back? What if he was dead, or in jail? But in the end, when someone you care about is looking at the end of life, they get to impose upon you. At least you tell them whatever they want to hear. "I promise," I finally said.

"Good, good." She closed her eyes, then slowly opened them. "Find him, Zack. And hurry. I don't know how long I can last."

Dale T. Phillips

CHAPTER 2

Allison had come with me from Maine, and I was trying to give us both a much-needed getaway. We'd only recently gotten back together, and I wanted some sunshine in our relationship. She'd never been to Florida, and though a sweaty summer is really not the time to be a tourist in Miami, she'd been happy to take some time off to join me. It was a good break from her job as nurse in the ER.

I'd also been eager to get away, thinking I could leave my problems behind. Problems like Ollie Southern, a biker gang leader who'd decided to engage me in a blood feud. He'd come close to having me killed, and went to prison for it. Then he was released by our game-show justice system, which gives criminals a free spin if they toss a bigger fish to the authorities. So now Ollie was out there somewhere, watching, waiting for his chance to kill me. He'd already burned down my martial arts dojo before it even opened.

I was tired of always looking over my shoulder, always watching the door to see who entered, always being cognizant of every pool of shadow. Here in sunny Miami, I thought I could finally relax for a change, and be reminded of why I was glad to be alive. Here death could back off awhile, and wait for that final dance.

But the Reaper was never far from my life. Mrs. Harris didn't have much time left, and the visit to the hospital had unnerved me. It was a small enough favor I could do for her, to grant her a bit of relief before death took her. But that meant cutting short my little vacation. Once again I'd have to disappoint Allison.

Back at the hotel, I looked for her. The shimmering sunlight and the reflection of the water in the hotel pool helped to push death a bit farther away, even if the display of slim, oiled, suntanned bodies in wisps of cloth looked like fish broiling in a pan. Allison was not among them. I found her on the hotel beach, under the shelter of a canopy that looked like half of a big dome tent. She reclined on a towel spread over a chaise lounge, wearing a blue bikini and huge round sunglasses. She held a tall glass that could have served as a vase. A paperback novel lay face down next to her. She looked much better than the slick, skinny, brown mannequins by the pool. She looked real and alive, and I needed that now.

"Hey," I said, pulling over another chaise lounge. "Enjoying yourself?"

"Immensely. I've always wanted to do this, just lie on a beach with a cool drink in my hand, and not a care in the world."

"Good."

She smiled. "Why don't you take your shirt off and relax with me?"

"I'm good." Apart from the jagged red slash above my eyebrow, I had an uglier scar on my abdomen, both souvenirs of my short stay in prison. People tended to stare.

I changed the subject. "How's the water?"

She wrinkled her nose. "Warm as piss. Not like Maine at all. It's like taking a bath in saltwater."

"Hope you used a lot of sunscreen. Sun's a lot stronger down here than what you're used to."

She hooked a finger onto a frame and blue eyes regarded me over the sunglasses. "I've seen too many skin cancer patients, so yes, I used proper protection. And you'll notice I'm in the shade now."

"Okay, don't get testy." I admired her legs, running a hand along her shin. "I just noticed you already have some color."

"That's not what you were noticing. But don't worry, I'll put aloe on."

I nodded at the glass. "Drinking before lunch?"

"Don't knock it, just because you don't partake. You know, I never liked the taste of coconut before, but a pina colada makes a wonderful mid-morning drink. See? Pineapple." She waved a small wedge of it on a little pink plastic sword, and popped it in her mouth. "Fruit's good for you."

I looked out at the water.

"What's the matter?" She took off her sunglasses.

"Nothing. Just a little sand in my eye."

She wasn't fooled. She set down the drink on a tray next to her and sat up. She reached over and gave me a hug. "It's okay."

"She was so full of life. It's hard to see her like that."

"I know. Believe me, I know. Sorry I didn't go with you. I just wanted a day away from a hospital."

Because she saw death on a daily basis, I hadn't asked her to go with me. "I thought she just wanted to say goodbye. But she wants me to find her grandson. He's her only relative, lives up in Maine."

Her eyebrows knitted together. "You going to play Don Quixote again?"

"They didn't part on the best of terms, and just lost contact. She thought I could get in touch with him, convince him to come back. I've got to go see her lawyer, get all the details."

"And of course you said you'd do it."

"I don't really want to, but she's just hanging on by a thread. I think she's only staying alive long enough to see him."

15

She studied my face for a bit. "Wait, let me guess. You want to leave right away."

My insides churned. "No, I don't want to leave. I'd like nothing better than a few days of R-and-R. I thought we'd have more time."

"Unbelievable." She threw up her hands.

"This is not what I want to do. The last time I tried to help somebody out with a personal problem, it almost cost me you." It was out before I could hold back. The previous Fall, Allison had asked me to help exonerate her cousin from a murder charge, and I'd almost been killed. Then she broke up with me because she couldn't stand the violence that hung about me like a curse.

She opened her mouth in surprise, and now it was her turn to have sand in her eyes. "Low blow there."

"Sorry." I couldn't take it back.

"Like hell you are." She swiped away some tears. "Still haven't forgiven me, have you?"

"Things got pretty bad, but having you back is all that matters."

We sat in silence for a time.

She sighed. "Some vacation. We come down here, and we're right back at it again."

"Look, I'll find the guy, and bring him to see her. You can come with me, and we can stay as long as we want."

"Sure." She didn't believe a word.

"Come on. She's not going to be around long. And to pay me for finding her grandson, she wants to leave me that painting I told you about."

"The Salvador Dali?"

"Yeah."

"There's a lot of fakes of his stuff, you know."

"It's real. She actually knew him. Met him after the war. She says it's worth something."

"Uh-huh."

I sat there feeling lousy, and wondering how to make it up to her. "You know," I said, rubbing my hands on my pants. "There's a whole Dali museum up in the Tampa-St. Pete area. I've always meant to get up there, but never have. Let's take a detour on our way back. We can catch a cheap flight, stay overnight. What do you say?"

She regarded me. "I'm thoroughly pissed at you. But I suppose I'll take the consolation prize."

"Let's have a nice lunch, then you can go shopping while I'm at the attorney's office."

"You're doing better, but still not out of the doghouse. And where'd you get all this money? Is it the insurance from your dojo fire?"

It would have been so easy to say yes. I had to lie anyway, as I'd liberated a bag of illicit cash from a drug dealer who was killed soon after. If I told her the truth, it would confirm that I was a law-breaking train wreck who attracted trouble like honey drew flies.

I shrugged. "It's my new security business."

She shook her head, knowing I was lying. "I don't know why I bother asking."

Dale T. Phillips

CHAPTER 3

I sweated my way along downtown Miami to the office of Saul Rabinowitz. He had a tasteful place, not overly gaudy or ostentatious, like much of Miami, but I didn't get to see it for long. When his receptionist announced me, he came right out, so he wasn't one of those jerks who kept someone waiting just to show how important he was.

He was short, balding, with a friendly face and a nice suit. I'd seen plenty of expensive threads in my days with the wealthy bad boys, and this one was a tailored job.

We made introductions and went to a well-cooled office with an excellent view of Biscayne Bay.

"Get you anything?" His voice was a touch high, but not unpleasant.

"No, thank you," I said.

"You've been to see Rita?"

I nodded. "This morning."

"Shame. Lovely lady. I've known her for years." He played with a folder that lay on his desk. "I take it you've agreed to look for Steven?"

I shrugged. "If it'll make her happy, I'll do what I can to get him down here."

He studied my face. "She thinks a lot of you. She trusts you for some reason."

Though the room was air-conditioned, it had just turned downright chilly. My radar went off. "And you don't?"

"In my line of work, I see a lot of people trying to take advantage of the elderly, trying to separate them from their money."

"Is this going somewhere?"

He tapped the folder. "You have quite an interesting history, Mr. Taylor." The friendly act was gone, the attorney in full attack mode. "It makes me suspicious. Damn suspicious. I don't see a lot of altruistic ex-cons."

My ears got a little hot. "And your reason for checking me out?"

"I take care of my clients. I have some the same age as her, some even older, very few as sharp. But there are a lot of people who prey on senior citizens, especially down here. Some of these older folks put their faith in people they shouldn't. I take it upon myself to see that they're protected from predators."

"And what's your verdict on me?"

He leaned forward. "I'm concerned that she's so trusting of someone who was in prison for aggravated assault. Care to comment?"

"Is this a cross-examination?"

"You going to plead the Fifth?"

"I'd like to tell you it's none of your damn business. Though I understand where you're coming from."

"Good." He sat back and picked up a gold pen, twirling it in his fingers. "So, what's your story?"

I sighed and told him about the bad old days of my youth, of my brief stint as a bodyguard for a former mob guy who didn't like guns. Long after I'd left that job, the federal authorities thought I might have information they could use. I didn't. I was never part of the crime organization. But one fed in particular roughed me up until I fought back. The fed wound up in the hospital, and I wound up in prison. Turned out the guy was dirty, and was indicted himself a short time later. I got out after a few months, but had some souvenirs of my stay: the scars on my body, and more on my soul.

I didn't mention my years of guilt and rage for the accidental death of my kid brother, and how that had driven me to almost kill myself by drinking. I left out a lot for Mr. Rabinowitz, but I gave him enough.

"And you took the room with Rita when you worked here." He looked thoughtful. "Where did you work?"

"Hernando's Hideaway. A club near Little Havana."

"I was there once or twice before it closed down. Nice place."

"If you contact Hernando, he can vouch for my character."

Rabinowitz put down the pen. "So Steven was working in Maine, and you live there now. Apart from that, what makes Rita think you can find him? Are you a private investigator?"

"You know damn well I'm not. With my past, no way I could get a license. But I've looked into some things for people, and I've got the time to do it."

"Seems like when you look into things, a lot of shit happens."

He certainly had been digging. "I see you found some old news stories."

"You have a way of finding trouble, don't you?"

I shrugged. "I left here to find out who killed my friend."

Rabinowitz studied me as if trying to peer into my soul. "It bothers me some. Quite a bit, actually. Despite your colorful past, you don't fit the mold of a usual con or crook. I know, I've seen quite a few. Rita didn't know you for very long, but wants you to have a valuable painting. I had to make sure you wouldn't just sell it. Maybe to buy drugs."

"Drugs? You've been in Miami too long."

"Probably, but where does an old Jew go to retire, when he's from here? No way am I going to Israel."

"Maine's nice."

"Hah. Like I should shovel snow, at my age?"

"So if I was going to sell the painting to buy drugs, how much could I buy?"

Rabinowitz started, but saw I was ribbing him. He shrugged. "It was appraised at just over a quarter of a million dollars."

I whistled. "That little thing? Why so much?"

"Apparently, it was supposed to go to one of Dali's lovers. But he gave it to Rita instead, and it caused a bit of a stir in their circles. When there's a good story, the price goes up."

"I don't even have a place to put it."

"Well, start looking. She certainly doesn't want Steven to get his grubby paws on it."

I cocked my head. "Not a fan?"

"Little bastard is a real pain in the ass. Rita took care of him after his parents died. No matter how much she gave, he wanted more. I kept telling her to cut him loose, the greedy shit. If she didn't want to see him so bad, I'd say don't bother finding him. Then he couldn't get the money, and it would all go to a good charity."

"What else do you know about him? Where do I start?"

Rabinowitz opened a drawer and took out a large document envelope with a flap. He slid it across the desk to me. "I tried to locate him, no luck. Everything's in there. Where he worked, last address, a couple of pictures."

"Thanks. I'll do what I can." He was still giving me an odd look. "Something else?"

"You haven't asked about expenses."

I shrugged. "I told you, I'm not a private eye. I don't get a per diem."

"Nevertheless, she wanted you to have something." He handed over a regular-sized envelope. Inside was a bunch of hundred-dollar bills. I looked up.

"Two thousand dollars," he said. "And if you need more, give me a call, but I'll want some kind of accounting, if that's the case."

"That's too much."

He shrugged. "She can afford it."

"She never struck me as wealthy."

"A lot people down here have got money squirreled away, yet you'd never know it by the way they live. And now you see why I wanted to check you out."

I smiled. "Usually, when I'm in a lawyer's office, it's me handing them a chunk of money."

He laughed. "Well, save it for next time, then. I'm sure you'll need it."

Dale T. Phillips

CHAPTER 4

Back in Maine, my reporter friend J.C. was there to pick us up when we landed at the Jetport, just outside the mall in South Portland.

"Good trip?" He smiled at Allison. "I see you got some color."

"Lovely time," she said, giving me a look. "Short as it was."

J.C. eyed the extra bags. "What's the matter? Run out of money?"

"Ha-ha," I said. "Help me with these. I think she bought half of South Beach."

"And we took a side trip and saw the Dali museum," Allison told him. "Those huge canvases. Amazing. Thanks, by the way, for giving us a lift."

"You'll have to buy me dinner," he said.

"Not if we're going anyplace with that expensive scotch you like," I said.

"Cheapskate."

"Tell you what. I'll buy you that scotch if you can help me with something. You know anybody in the art world? Silly question. Of course you do, you know everybody. Know any art dealers in Ogunquit?"

"A few. Look at you. You go to one museum, and now you're buying art."

"I have to look somebody up. Grandson of a friend of mine. The one I went down to Florida for. She wants to see him before she goes. He worked at a gallery in Ogunquit, and they lost touch. The place didn't keep track of him, so I'll have to ask around. People will talk more if they know someone you know."

J.C. frowned and shook his head. "The last person I had check into something for you didn't do so well."

"I'm sorry. Didn't know running a license plate was going to force a guy into early retirement. How does he like it?"

"It's all right. He likes to fish, and gets to do it a couple of years earlier, thanks to the little boat you paid for."

"Do I want to know any of this?" Allison sighed.

"Guy stuff," I said.

She looked disgusted. "So where are we eating?"

"I know this nice little place," said J.C.

"Of course you do."

The restaurant in Portland was indeed both nice and little, having only eight tables. They served elegant Italian meals, with linen tablecloths and all the fancy trimmings. It was one of those places where the staggering prices weren't shown on the menu. I grimaced at J.C. "I was thinking of something more like a good burger."

He shrugged. "My fees are in line with my services. Besides, you were just living it up down south with fine dining. Why shouldn't I have some?"

"Oh, yeah, Miami in the summer. What could be better?"

Allison gave me a light smack. "It was a good time. Could have been longer."

"Sure, you sunned on the beach, drank rum, and shopped. I went to a hospital and a lawyer's office."

"So why'd you hurry back?" said J.C.

"The White Knight has another mission," Allison said. "He's on the hunt again. I suppose it'll get him out of his funk. He's been mopey ever since the fire, doesn't know what to do with himself."

I shrugged. "She doesn't have much time, so I have to find him and drag him back."

"Well, it's not like you have a lot of other things on your plate." J.C. peered at me over his glasses.

"Ouch. Et tu, Brute? Actually, I'll have you know, I'm in a new line of work." I handed him one of my spiffy business cards. "They came in just before I left."

He read from the card. "Zack Taylor, Security Consultant. Keeping you and yours safe." He looked at Allison. "Tell me you didn't help him with this."

She shook her head. "All his idea. Hey, I want some wine. I'm still on vacation."

She ordered a bottle of pinot noir, J.C. ordered his fancy scotch, and I had my usual club soda with a lime. Allison was drinking a lot more than usual, but I decided not to say anything at the time.

J.C. scanned the menu. "So how are you going to find this person?"

"Her attorney called the gallery where he worked, and they say he's not there anymore, no idea where he went. It may be a dead end, but I'm going to check it out. See where he lived, ask around. He was an artist, so maybe I can find some other artists. Maybe somebody knows something. He dropped a hint once that he needed money, and might do a fake painting or two to raise some cash."

"Ah. So maybe he doesn't want to be found."

"Maybe not. And maybe that's why the gallery said they didn't know. Then it's a different story. People might lie for him. If they do, then I'll know, and I'll have a place to start."

Allison looked at me and took a gulp of wine. "I can lie right to your face, and you have no clue." She and J.C. shared a conspiratorial look.

"That's different. I want to believe you."

She snorted.

I ignored her, and went on. "Liars give themselves away in a number of ways. You get them talking, and then ask them a pointed question. If they lie, something will change: their face, their body language, their voice, their speech patterns. Your gut tells you when something is off. When I worked door security and bodyguard detail, I learned to spot the tics."

"What if no one really knows where he is?"

"Then I have a lot more work to do."

CHAPTER 5

Ogunquit was a tourist town on the southern Maine coast, not far from Portland. The name supposedly means "beautiful place by the sea" in the Abenaki language. Lots of places in Maine held their native names, even though it was often difficult to find original natives. This village was an artists' mecca, and had been so since the end of the 1800s. It seemed to have hundreds of galleries and restaurants to serve the tourist trade, most of them aimed at the higher-end visitor. Not for these folks the sweaty pier and working-class carnival atmosphere of Old Orchard Beach; no, here was The Money, and they made sure you damn well knew it.

On this fine Summer day, the tourists were many, and parking was a problem. I didn't mind the long walk from the distant lot where I finally found a spot. I wore my best suit. Actually, it was my only suit.

Following directions, I made my way to the Oswego Gallery. When I walked in, a bell attached to the door sounded a soft silvery chime. The place had the aroma of a fancy scented candle.

An attractive young woman came over and smiled at me. It was a genuine one, and I smiled back.

Her voice was soft. She couldn't have been much over twenty. "Can I help you, sir?"

"I hope so. I'm looking for Mr. Abernathy."

"Who shall I say is calling?"

I handed her one of my new business cards. She studied it.

"Something amiss, miss?"

She looked up, and flushed a light pink. "Sorry, no."

"You can be honest. I won't be offended."

"It's a nice format, but I would have used a different font, and a darker shade for the background."

"Art and design student, I take it."

"Guilty," she said. "I didn't mean—"

"It's okay. What's your name?"

"Rebecca."

"Not a problem, Rebecca."

"I'll go get Mr. Abernathy."

I was glad I'd got the new Summer help. She hadn't made me state my business, so I could surprise Abernathy. Better if he wasn't prepared for it.

When a man came out, Rebecca discreetly let us alone to talk. Abernathy was about five-five, and sported a gray ponytail and meticulously trimmed Van Dyke beard. His suit looked custom-made. And his shoes weren't off-the-rack either. Italian-made, most likely, and definitely hand-stitched. Nice.

But his face was stern, and his tone was flat, dismissive. "Whatever you're selling, I'm not interested." No handshake, no pleasantries.

Something about Abernathy had set off my internal radar. "I'm not selling anything. I'm looking for Steven Harris."

A look of surprise flitted across Abernathy's features, followed by another one of calculation as his eyes narrowed. "What's this about?"

"As you can see from my card, I'm a security consultant. It's a security matter." I smiled. Vague and just a trifle ominous.

"He doesn't work here anymore."

"Why's that?"

"Excuse me?" Now Abernathy looked confused.

"Why doesn't he work here anymore?"

"Well, I ... he left, that's all I can tell you." His gaze shifted from side to side.

"Did he leave on good terms?"

"Well, yes, of course. Why are you asking? Is there a problem?"

"You could say that." I decided to play the bluff. "He sold my client a painting."

"We sell a great many paintings here."

"This one was a fake."

Abernathy flinched, then recovered, drawing himself up to his full five-foot-five. "We do not sell art forgeries."

"Well, this guy did, in this gallery, and the bill of sale is on your letterhead. That's why I'd like to talk to him, see if we can settle the matter without any fuss, or outside agencies. You must know where to reach him."

"I'm afraid I don't."

"No forwarding address? No word about where he was going?"

"I really didn't know him that well."

"But you hired him. He give you a resume?"

"I don't– that is, we don't have such things." Little beads of sweat were popping out on Abernathy's forehead. The air was cool in here, so it wasn't the temperature.

I smiled. "You hired a person you didn't know, without a resume?"

"He had an MFA, and was recommended by a good friend of mine."

"May I speak with this friend?"

He stiffened. "I'm afraid not. She values her privacy."

"Maybe some of your staff knew him better. Perhaps I could talk with them."

I could almost see the wheels spinning. "No one else here knew him, either."

"I see." I paused, letting the silence build up. "Then I suppose my client has no choice but to get the police involved. We were hoping to keep this a private matter, but I suppose they're better equipped to deal with this."

Abernathy made a show of deliberating. "How much did your client pay for this painting?"

"Five thousand. It must seem like a great deal of fuss for such a small sum."

"We would of course prefer that the gallery not be associated with any alleged impropriety on the part of our employees. If your client would be willing to bring in the painting and his sale sheet, I think we could come to an arrangement."

"You'd buy it back?" I smelled a rat, which was *art* spelled differently.

"If we can verify everything, yes."

"I'll convey your offer. Thank you for your time."

"I'll show you out."

I'd baited my hook with a complete lie, and somehow had got it in good. My pulse was racing, and I felt better than I had since my dojo burned down.

CHAPTER 6

Down the street, a coffee shop with outdoor tables had a good view of the Oswego gallery. I wanted a simple coffee, to have an excuse to stake out the gallery, but the brew here was gourmet, the menu board had at least two sentences to describe each kind, and a small cup cost me almost the price of a regular lunch in Portland. Ah, the tourist trade. I took my pricey java and sat where I could see the ocean on one side and the gallery on the other.

After about fifteen minutes or so, Abernathy came out. I followed him, but there were so many tourists crowding the sidewalks and streets, I lost him in a crush a few minutes later. I blamed it on him, for being so short.

Now what? I thought of the young lady at the gallery. She might know something, so I needed a reason to chat with her. As I headed back to the Oswego, I passed an upscale candy shop. It gave me an idea, and I made a stop before continuing on.

The gallery door chimed as before, and Rebecca came out on cue.

"Hi there," I said. "I need to ask Mr. Abernathy one more thing."

"Oh, he just stepped out."

"Ah, nuts." I looked around. "This means I have to stay in town for a bit. I picked up these chocolates from the shop down the street for later, but it's so hot out, they'll melt. I hate to see them go to waste. You like chocolate?"

Rebecca smiled. "Seaside Sweets. My favorite."

"Enjoy, then."

She took the box with four little truffles inside. Such a trusting young lady, taking candy from a stranger. She opened it and plucked one out. "These are sooo good." She popped the truffle in her mouth, and her smile got wider. "Mmmm."

"They certainly looked good. Did Mr. Abernathy say anything after I left?"

"He seemed a little upset, made a couple of phone calls. He closed the door, so I didn't really hear anything."

"He told me that there was a young man, Steven, who had worked here. Did you know him?"

"No, but one of the other girls said I was his replacement."

"Did she say anything about him or his leaving?"

"Just that Mr. Abernathy told the staff it was a family problem."

Except I knew Steven's family consisted of one grandmother, who he didn't talk to. "When was that?"

"I came on in May, after school got out." She was eyeing the other three truffles. "I better save these for later." She smiled at me. "What kind of security do you do?"

"All kinds."

"Do you have a gun?" Her voice was a little husky. Uh-oh.

"No. Don't like them."

Her brow wrinkled just a tad. "Isn't that kind of a drawback for security work?"

I smiled. "Not really. Guns give people a false sense of security. I give them the real thing."

"Oh." There was the faintest pink flush at her throat.

"For example, you don't have any visible cameras. It's a good deterrent."

"Well, we have an alarm system, of course."

"Interior motion detectors?"

"Uh, I'm not sure. But there's not much crime here. The police patrol pretty regularly."

In a town with this much wealth, I bet they did. I pressed on. "Mr. Abernathy was telling me about his friend who recommended Steven. I forgot her name."

"Probably Mrs. Perkins. She's in here all the time."

"That's it," I snapped my fingers. "How do I get in touch with her?"

"She sponsors a local art colony. We've got some brochures. Let me get you one."

Sweet, guileless young thing. I felt bad about taking advantage of her. She came back a moment later with a glossy trifold and handed it to me.

I looked it over. "This is the address where Steven got his mail."

"Then he was probably one of the artists. They apply for a grant to live there for a time, while they produce something. It's smaller than some places, like the MacDowell, and not as well known. And they only take visual artists: painters, sculptors, photographers and such. No writers, or poets, or musicians."

"Rebecca, you've been extremely helpful. Thank you."

"Well, thank you for the chocolate."

"My pleasure. Say, if I upset Mr. Abernathy with questions, I'm sorry. I don't want to get you into trouble with him, so maybe we shouldn't bother telling him about my return. Besides," I said, trying a little too hard to sell it, "he might want some of those truffles."

She nodded and smiled again, seeming not to suspect a thing. "I'm here all Summer, so stop by anytime."

Dale T. Phillips

CHAPTER 7

Allison's voice over the phone sounded surprised. "You want me to go with you where?"

"The Colony. An artist's retreat near Ogunquit."

"I've heard of it. You're looking for that guy there?"

"Or any trace of him. He was probably an artist in residence at some point, so maybe someone knows where he is now."

"What do you need me for?"

"I want a beautiful woman beside me to distract people."

"I see."

"You seemed to have a good time at the museum, so I thought maybe you'd like this. Hey, it's an artist colony, and you love art. And it's a gorgeous day out."

"What else?"

"You can keep me out of trouble."

"I thought so." There was a pause. "I do have to work later."

"We can check the place out, have a nice dinner, and I'll have you back in time for work."

She finally agreed. I buzzed back up to Portland to get her. I took the turnpike, as Route 1 in the Summer was pretty much a traffic nightmare.

Allison was looking at the brochure as I drove. "It looks nice. This was a dream of mine once, you know. Get your expenses paid to just paint all day. Then talk to other artists at night."

"Doesn't pay as well as nursing."

"A lot less death, though. Prettier, too. Calmer."

She looked out the window, and was quiet. I wondered if she was reminded of lost opportunities, and suddenly wasn't so sure this was a good idea.

We got off the turnpike and drove inland a few miles, following the directions in the brochure. We came to a tree-lined driveway with a gate, flanked by stone pillars. The gate was open, so I drove in and parked by a small building with a sign that read "Visitor's Center."

Inside was a fifty-ish woman with short blonde hair. She smiled at us. "Hello. Welcome to the Colony. Have you been here before?"

Allison spoke. "No. We wanted to see what it was like."

"I can show you around, if you'd like. I'm Peggy."

"That would be nice. I'm Allison, he's Zack." She indicated the small easel set up behind the desk. "Are you an artist?"

"Yes. I volunteer here, because I can work and still answer phones and such."

"We didn't want to interrupt."

"Don't worry, I'm just practicing. It's nothing special." Peggy came out from behind the desk. "Besides, it's good to get up and stretch every now and again."

We walked outside, and Peggy rattled off the history of the place, and the names of some of the folk who had passed through these doors. I didn't recognize any of them. She pointed out cottages hidden behind screens of trees, and said that no one was allowed to go near each occupied cabin during the day, except for a person who quietly and unobtrusively delivered a lunch basket. At night, most of the artists in residence would gather in the group dining hall for dinner and discussion.

Because Peggy seemed so charmed by Allison, I held off on my questions and kept my mouth shut for a change. Peggy took us to the gallery, where I saw works for sale from past and present members, and a few items to constitute the gift shop end.

We looked at the art on display. Allison walked slowly past the first set of pictures, then the second. She wrinkled her nose.

"Something wrong?" Peggy looked at her.

"No, it's just ... I hate to sound critical, but some are modern art pastiches and some are, well, to be kind, derivative. I mean that one is a straight ripoff of Kandinsky."

Peggy smiled. "You're not hurting my feelings. I agree with you. We have a few poseurs here. Some are barely a notch or two above the seascape painters who knock out beach scenes for tourists. We're not talking Academy level by any means."

Allison came to the next one, a large, striking portrait of a woman. "This one is really nice."

"Good taste. It's mine."

"Really? It's a great use of white to bring out character. The way Sargent would put a bold stroke of white that just drew your eye in."

"You have a great eye," said Peggy. "Do you paint?"

"Used to. A long time ago." I could hear a touch of sadness in her voice. She moved on. There was a series of photos, huge irregular blotches, like giant Rorschach blots. "What are these?"

"Leeches. Gregory keeps tanks of them and photographs them. You should see them sometime. It's hypnotizing, like watching a lava lamp."

We passed more sets of paintings and came to a display of metal cast-off parts that had been welded into shapes. There was some fun and funky stuff. It was interesting to see how the sculptor had fused pieces of different things together to make something new.

"These are Adam's," Peggy said. "He's got the most talent of all of us. He's a blacksmith, and is always finding scraps of things to put together. He makes good money selling his works, and they're popular, so the others are wicked jealous."

Peggy touched Allison's arm. "Want to meet everyone? We start gathering in that hall over there in a few minutes. Can't invite you to dinner after, but you'd have an hour to meet and greet."

Allison looked at me. "Why not?" I said.

Peggy led us to the dining hall on the other side of the compound. There was an open area inside, with round tables that sat eight at each one. A huge stone fireplace dominated one end of the room, and couches and comfy chairs popped up here and there.

"There's Adam," Peggy said, and took us over to meet him. He was tall and brawny, with a mane of golden-brown hair and beard. He held a tall glass of amber beer, was remarkably soft-spoken for such a big guy, and seemed pleasant enough. Peggy told him we'd liked his work, and he thanked us. After a few minutes of chitchat, he excused himself to go speak to someone about getting some tanks refilled so he could do more welding.

"Over there is Marissa," Peggy said.

"We're not going over to meet her?"

"Believe me, I'm doing you a favor. She's a total bitch. Got the artistic temperament, without the talent."

"What about him?"

"Robert Emerson. We can meet him, if you want. He'll spend the whole time looking down his nose at you, so you'll get a good view of his nostrils."

Allison chuckled. "Is there anybody likable here besides you and Adam?"

Peggy smiled. "Most of the real artists are still working. Those two like to talk about work, but don't do a lot of it. There's Bennett and Cecily. They're nice. Let's go meet them."

I was eager to ask questions, but Allison seemed to be enjoying herself, and it didn't seem like the right time. I was hoping for an opening in the conversation, a chance to drop Steven's name. A few more minutes went by, and there was nothing. It would soon be time for dinner, when we'd have to go. I peeled Peggy aside.

"Can I ask you something?"

"Sure," she said. "Seems like you've been wanting to do that for some time."

"I have," I said. "I'm trying to be polite."

Over her shoulder, I saw Abernathy enter. Beside him was an elderly lady on the arm of a huge guy in a suit, with dark sunglasses on.

Abernathy pointed at me. "What the hell are you doing here?"

The room went very quiet.

"I told you. Looking for Steven."

"You can't come here like this."

"We were just looking around."

"I think you're trying to start trouble." He turned to the elderly woman. "Loretta, he's trespassing." He indicated the man-mountain. "Tell Roger to get him out of here."

The big guy looked down at the lady, and she nodded. He disengaged from her, and moved in my direction. People parted to give him a wide berth. I sighed. Hands up, palms out, I smiled. "Okay, we're going. No worries."

The guy grabbed my collar anyway, and started dragging me.

"Let go," I said. "I already said I was leaving." No response. "You'd better stop there, fella. This is assault and battery. I'm being attacked." I said that to cover myself for what I was about to do. If the police got involved, people had heard my words, and that would offer me a little protection with the law. The room was abuzz.

"Quiet everyone," said Abernathy. "This man is trespassing."

"I'm trying to leave. Tell him to get his hands off me. He's choking me."

I reached up for the arm that held me, grabbed his thick wrist in one hand, and levered the arm up at the elbow, with my other hand behind the joint. His hold loosened, and I twisted, pulling down and away. He gasped, and I straightened his arm out with him bent over.

"You going to call him off now?"

"Roger," said the elderly lady. "Let the man leave."

He grunted, and I shoved him onto a couch. He came up off the couch and turned with his hands up in a fighting stance, like he wanted to go another round.

"Roger." The woman's voice rang out in the once-more quiet room. He put his hands down, and spoke low to me, so she couldn't hear. "Another time, then."

In the car, I could tell Allison was pissed again. "Take me home."

"What about dinner?"

"Just take me home."

CHAPTER 8

Although I'd found a connection between the gallery where Steven had worked and the artists' colony, I was unlikely to be invited back to either. By rare good fortune, it was Peggy who answered when I called the next day.

"Hey, sorry about what happened," I said.

"Wow. That was the most fun we've had in a while. Everybody was abuzz."

"What did they tell you about me?"

"They said we shouldn't talk to you. That you were snooping around, trying to cause trouble."

"I was, in a way. I'd been to Abernathy's gallery earlier in the day. He acted squirrelly when I mentioned Steven Harris's name. I came to the colony to see if anyone knew where Steven was, or could give me more information. Then Abernathy shows up and declares me an enemy of the people."

"What about Steven?"

"His grandmother is a friend of mine. She's down in Miami, dying of cancer, and wants to see him again. She's a tough old gal, but she doesn't have a lot of time. She lost contact, and I said I'd look for him."

There was silence on the other end. "Peggy?"

"Is that what you were going to talk to me about?"

"Yeah, what's the big secret?"

A sigh. "There's some stuff going on."

"Can I buy you lunch and talk about it?"

"Okay, but not around here. I don't want to take the chance of being spotted with you. They might revoke my grant."

"How about Portland, then? You know where DeMillo's is?"

"I do, and I approve."

"See you at twelve thirty, then, how's that?"

"Good. But one more thing."

"What?"

"Bring Allison."

I chewed my lip. "She's not real pleased with me right now."

"She'll get over it. Bring her along."

Allison took a bit of convincing. Luckily it was another nice day, and we could sit by the water and watch the boats. Allison drank wine and looked at me with narrowed eyes from time to time.

"Hey, you two," Peggy said, joining us. "You sure know how to make an exit."

"Hope I didn't get you into any trouble," I said.

Peggy waved her hand. "They threw a few questions at me, but didn't seem to think we were buds or anything." She looked at Allison. "Is that wine good?" Allison slid her glass over, and Peggy took a sip. "Yum. I'll have one too." She beamed at Allison.

"So what's the big deal with Steven?"

Peggy leaned back. "It's not just him, there's other stuff going on."

"For instance?"

"How about a war?"

"What?"

"An art war."

Of course the waiter chose that moment to arrive. Peggy ordered her wine, and I could barely wait until the waiter was out of earshot. "Who's fighting?"

"Our own Mrs. Perkins, who you saw last night, and the Holloway brothers."

"And they are?"

"Identical twins. From away. British, I heard. They own the biggest gallery, and a lot of others. They want to control everything, and they're ruthless. Mrs. Perkins is old-line Maine family, and is a dear, really, and wants to help artists."

"Perkins is a pretty solid name in these parts," Allison said. "She related to the Perkins of Perkins Cove?"

"Distant cousin."

"I'm surprised they'd let outsiders get a foothold."

"The Holloways are resourceful, and seems like they stop at nothing. And money talks. With them, it talks big. When they started, they were just another gallery. Now they've got a reach."

I cut in. "So what's involved?"

"Control of the market and the art scene here along the coast. Ownership of what gets sold, and to who, which galleries succeed and which fail, who gets into certain auctions. Millions of dollars at stake, even here, so far from New York. And of course, battles over the artists, pulling them into one camp or the other. They're used like chess pawns."

"Anything go beyond dirty tricks into actual illegal acts?" I was looking for the kind of handle I could turn to put the pressure on.

Just then the waiter came back with Peggy's wine, and I had to wait once again for her answer.

She took a sip and continued. "It's said the Holloways are into a lot of stuff: bribery, extortion, drugs, anything and everything. Mrs. Perkins had to hire a bodyguard after there were some threats. And then there was Owen."

"Who's that?"

"Artist at our colony. Drowned a few months ago. Body was found out in the ocean by some fishermen."

"Accident?"

"That's the official verdict. But I think there was something else going on. Owen wasn't much for boats."

Allison groaned.

Peggy looked startled. "Did I say something wrong?"

"It's him," Allison waved her hand at me. "I thought he was just trying to find someone. But now there's a war, a mystery, and a dead body. He loves that shit. Now he'll be like a bloodhound on the trail."

Peggy looked at me.

I shrugged. "Guilty."

The waiter was back yet again, and Allison ordered a bottle of wine. I gave her a look, but didn't say anything. I had to pretend to be patient through the uncorking process. Allison approved it after a tasting sip, Peggy and she got their glasses filled, and finally we were by ourselves again.

I turned back to Peggy. "So how does Steven fit into all this?"

"He had a grant and was out at the colony, same as the rest of us. He had some talent, but was better at copying something another artist had done, less so on anything original. He had a boyfriend in town here, another artist. Bosco St. Clair."

I raised my eyebrows. She shrugged. "Yeah, dumbass made-up name, but that's what he calls himself. Was a too-frequent visitor at the colony. Then he started riding the white horse."

"Heroin?"

"Yup. Parties got a little wild, if you know what I mean. Mrs. Perkins found out and went apeshit. Steven was gone the next day. From the gallery, too. He was Abernathy's fair-haired boy, but he's dead to them now. Maybe that's why they don't know where he is."

"Hmm. What about the boyfriend?"

"I see him around from time to time, but no one from the colony is friendly with him, as far as I know. He wasn't the most well-liked guy to start with, and the drugs just made it worse."

"Sounds like he could be a lead. Any idea where I could find him?"

"How connected are you with the gay life here in Portland?"

I shrugged. "Not at all."

"Need a little help with that?"

I thought about it. "I don't want word getting back that you're helping me, put your grant in any danger."

"Let me make a few calls. See what I can do. Although it would probably help to find Bosco if you sold heroin."

Dale T. Phillips

CHAPTER 9

Peggy and I wound up bar-hopping later that night. We were sitting in a place where the art crowd crossed paths with the gay subculture. The only thing I minded was that people were drinking and having a good time. I'd been able to hang out in bars when I could shut myself off and not care about anything. Now it was like an ache from an old war wound.

Peggy waved her hand. "A lot of the students from the Maine College of Art hang out here, as do some of my friends. Bosco is usually either here, or one other place. He's kind of high-profile. Somebody will know. Just be patient." She looked at me. "Are you gonna be okay if you get hit on?"

"I think I'll be fine. I lived in Miami."

"Be great if you found someone, though. Leave my path clear, know what I mean?"

We watched the crowd for a few minutes, Peggy sipping her drink, and me nursing my club soda. She excused herself and went up to a knot of people at the bar. She came back a few minutes later.

"They said he's probably at the other place. Want to go? It's not far."

We arrived at the other bar five minutes later, and went inside. There was a good crowd, and we went to the far side, scanning the room.

"There he is. Wait here," Peggy said. She walked over to a table of five, and I saw her bend down to talk to someone. She came back with a man in tow, tall, thin, with a hawk-nosed face. He wore a silver hoop through one earlobe, and had a stud in one eyebrow.

"Bosco, this is Zack. Zack, Bosco."

"Charmed, I'm sure." Bosco extended his hand palm down, bent at the wrist, like a lady offering it to be kissed. I didn't kiss it. He smirked. "Peggy, we haven't seen you in ages. What's up at that stuffy old place?"

"Oh, you know, same old, same old. How about you? What trouble have you been up to?"

"All kinds of wickedness." Bosco shot me a look like he was seeing how I'd react.

"Hey, you ever talk to Stevie?"

The temperature in the room seemed to drop as Bosco immediately lost the friendly act and the affected speech. He stared directly at Peggy. "Why are you asking about him?"

"Oh, you know. Just wondering how he made out. You two still an item?"

He tried for nonchalant and didn't make it. "No, doll, haven't seen Stevie in forever. So why are you hanging out with this hunk? Is he a new toy for me?"

"He says Stevie's grandma down in Florida is dying and wants to see him."

Bosco flinched as if slapped.

"What's the matter?" Peggy was doing all the work for me.

"Nothing. Listen, I have to make a phone call, something very important. I'll be back in a flash." He scuttled off and went to the pay phone on the back wall.

I looked at Peggy. "I'd say we rattled his cage pretty good. Wonder who he's calling."

I watched Bosco as he made the call. He carefully avoided looking in our direction. He was on for some time, at least ten minutes. When he was done, he finally looked at us, shrugged, and pointed first to himself and then in the direction of the men's room. He stopped to chat on his way there, sneaking looks at us. When he was out of sight, I turned to Peggy. "I'm guessing this place has a back door. He's bugging out."

She smiled. "Need any help running down the little shit?"

"Nah. I got it."

I took off out the front door and around the side. I found the alley behind the place, and almost bowled Bosco over as he tried to hurry away. "We didn't finish our talk," I said, grabbing a handful of his jacket. His face had the look of a frightened rabbit.

"Leave me alone," he said. "You don't know what you're messing with."

"No, I don't," I admitted. "That's why I need some information from you. Why is asking about Stevie so scary?"

"I don't know where he is. I haven't seen him."

"You're a terrible liar, Bosco. Just tell me. Is he in some kind of trouble?"

"You are." The voice came from behind me.

I turned, moving Bosco between me and the speaker. A rather large man was coming toward us, flexing his fists. He looked like two days' worth of bad news.

"I'm just asking about a friend of his," I said. I wasn't completely sure this wasn't one of Bosco's acquaintances thinking I was simply bullying a gay man. But if it had been a buddy, Bosco would have relaxed more. He still looked panicked.

"Too bad for you, then."

I pushed Bosco toward the guy to see how the man would react. He brushed Bosco aside and kept coming. I turned slightly, adjusting my balance.

When I judged he was close enough, I snapped out a kick to his knee, and followed with a smack to his nose after my kick brought his head forward. I front-kicked with the other leg, low so he couldn't grab me. Now my left was facing him, and I fired a pair of jabs that brought his hands up to defend his face. I threw a solid hook into his now-open gut, knocking him back, but not down. Tough bastard.

Before he could recover, I drove another side-kick to his kneecap, and got a groan, but he slipped back out of range. Fast learner.

A sound made me stop. It was the slide of an automatic. I looked past the attacker, and there stood another man, almost as big, holding his weapon in a classic shooter's stance, sights trained on my center mass. "Enough," was all he said. There was nowhere to get away in the alley. Palms up, I backed off.

The injured man hissed to his compatriot. "Do it. Outside this club, they'll write it off."

I heard a door open behind me. "Zack? You out here?"

"Go back inside." I doubted the guy would want to pop us both, but he had to shoot her if he shot me. Instead, the gunman grabbed his wounded buddy and disappeared. I started breathing again. I looked around, but Bosco had flown the coop.

Peggy came back out. "Did that guy have a gun on you?"

"He sure did."

"What was all that about?"

"Seems our boy Bosco called in the cavalry."

CHAPTER 10

I called J.C. "I just had an interesting run-in with a pair of mooks. One pulled a gun."

He sighed. "Old friends, or new ones?"

"New ones."

"You have a knack."

"I asked an artist about Stevie, and he ran off to the phone, made a call, and bolted. I grabbed him, but two tough guys showed up."

"And you called me why?"

"I heard about an art war going on locally. I wondered how serious it got."

"Well, it's not the mob wars in Chicago," J.C. said. "This is the first I've heard about gunmen."

"Someone from the art colony drowned a few months ago."

"Oh, yes. I heard about that. It was a friend of Sonny's that pulled him from the water."

"Our friend Sonny, the giant lobsterman?"

"The same."

"Think I could talk to him?"

"Well, tomorrow's Sunday, and Sonny's hosting a clambake. I'm going, and I can call and see if his friend will be there. You like clams and lobster?"

"Lobster, yeah, not so much on the clams. But Allison likes both."

"Bring her along. Sonny will like her."

"But will she like Sonny?"

"They'll get along famously. Let me make a call and I'll get back to you."

The next day, Allison and I joined J.C. on the ferry out to Peak's Island, the giant jewel of Casco Bay. J.C. had his car on board, and we stood at the rail on a glorious Maine Summer day. The water was a palette of iridescent colors shimmering in the light. I felt the ocean breeze and exulted in the warmth of the sun.

"This is nice," Allison said. "I hope it turns out better than the last outing you took me on."

J.C. looked at me. I shrugged. "We went to the art colony down near Ogunquit. The gallery owner recognized me and had some guy try to throw us out. It wasn't my fault."

J.C. shook his head. "You find more trouble in a day than most people find in a lifetime."

I ignored him and addressed Allison. "As good as Miami?"

"Better," she said. "This is home."

"My home, too, now."

"Sure you're not just another flatlander tourist?"

"That hurts."

"You wave at the other boats. That's what tourists do."

"They waved at us first. And I'm happy."

J.C. snorted and moved off down the rail.

I enjoyed the rest of the voyage, and we all piled into the car when we reached the dock. We finally got through the milling masses at the landing, and headed across the island. Peaks was prime real estate now, but Sonny's family had lived here for several generations. We pulled into a driveway filled with beat-up trucks, new Volvos, and half a dozen motorcycles. The bikes gave me a start, but they ran to sporty models. None looked like the type favored by the biker gang that wanted me dead.

There was quite a festive crowd when we went around out back. J.C. caught Sonny's eye and waved. We made our way through the knots of people. Sonny was on the back deck at a giant grill, cooking hamburgers and hot dogs, with a spatula in one hand and a bottle of beer in the other. J.C. took Allison's hand and brought her forward. "Allison, this is your erstwhile host, Sonny. Sonny, this is the beautiful Allison. And you remember Zack."

Sonny looked at Allison. He jerked his head toward me. "You could do better, you know."

"I know. But he brings me to the best places," she spread her hands, and they both laughed.

J.C. looked at the grill. "Some clambake."

"This is for the kiddies, and those pussies who won't eat lobster and clams. Merrill's tending the bake."

"Merrill is Sonny's brother," J.C. explained. "The nice one."

"Only 'cause he hardly says a goddamned word," Sonny said, and turned a line of burgers. He looked around. "Doobie! Get your ass over heah and make yourself useful." Sonny's Down East accent was fun to listen to, like an old Marshall Dodge '*Bert and I*' routine.

A rangy fellow with a Red Sox cap came over, beer in hand. Sonny handed him the spatula.

"You tend this meat, and don't you let it burn."

Doobie nodded, and took over without a word. Sonny finished his beer. "Come with me," he said, placing his empty bottle in a barrel. He started for the house and we followed him inside.

Setting off the living room was a big painting on the wall, framed well, with good lighting. We all stopped to look at it.

"Looks like a Hartley," Allison said.

"You got a good eye, sweetie," said Sonny, beaming. "My grandaddy knew old Marsden, would take him out fishin' once in a while. We got a coupla others around the place, but this is our pride and joy." Sonny looked at me. "What's the matter? You don't think a boat bum like me knows good art?"

"I wonder how many lobstermen have a museum-quality piece worth thousands hanging on their wall," I said.

"Not too goddamn many, I'll betcha," Sonny laughed. "All right, J.C. let me get out the good stuff." Sonny went to a small bar set in a nook. He set out three squat glasses and put a bottle of scotch up on the bar. "You gonna have some, darlin'?"

"No thanks," said Allison. "I'll have some white wine, though."

"Comin' right up," Sonny said. He took a glass away and replaced it with a wine goblet. He reached into a cooler behind the bar and came up with a tall, slim bottle. "Pinot grigio?"

"Lovely," said Allison.

Sonny retrieved a corkscrew and opened the wine. He poured a generous amount into the wine glass and handed it to Allison. He looked at me. "Juice box for you?"

"Funny, Sonny."

He opened a bottle of club soda and poured some into a tall glass. "Ice?"

"No, thanks."

He put a wedge of lime into the glass and pushed it across the bar.

I looked at it. "You cut fresh limes?"

"We're havin' a goddamned party, ain't we?"

Sonny opened the scotch and poured into the two glasses. When he was done, about a third of the bottle was gone. J.C. took one glass and held it up to the light. He nodded and clinked glasses with Sonny. He took a sip and stood there with his eyes closed in an almost reverent pose.

Since he looked so enthralled, I couldn't help commenting. "Should we be singing the Hallelujah Chorus?"

"Shush," he said. "We are in the presence of greatness."

"Not too shabby," said Sonny. "At a hunnert bucks a bottle, it oughta be. Only trouble is, now I can't drink beer for a while. Don't want to drown this out."

"Small price to pay," said J.C.

"The wine's good, too," said Allison. Sonny smiled at her.

I held up my club soda. "Party on. You live pretty good for a fisherman, Sonny."

"That's 'cause I never got married," said Sonny. "Lemme go find Lewis." He left, while we stood around and sipped our drinks.

J.C. smiled at Allison. "He really likes you. Not many get this kind of treatment. He certainly wouldn't have rolled out the red carpet for him." He indicated me with a motion of his head.

"I'm flattered," Allison said. "This is the second time this week Zack has pimped me out as bait. Last time it was a woman, though."

J.C. raised his eyebrows.

I shrugged. "After we were asked to leave the art colony, I needed to talk to someone there. She asked if Allison could come along. So we all had a nice meal."

"And I take it her interest was more romantic than sisterly," J.C. said.

"I'm surprised he doesn't have me dress more hookerish. You know, boots, low-cut blouse, lots of makeup. Anything to get information."

"Hey," I said. "J.C. was the one who said to bring you today."

"See? You're all in on it."

"And you make the best honeytrap ever, my dear," said J.C.

I was looking at Allison, but she didn't seem truly upset. And she had a point, which I didn't want to admit.

Sonny came back with a grizzled old fisherman, whose skin was as tanned as a saddle, and with wrinkles around his eyes from squinting into the sun for too many years. He wore rumpled old clothes, but they looked clean and didn't smell of fish.

"This here's Lewis," Sonny said, before pointing at the rest of us in turn. "Allison, J.C., and Zack."

"How do," Lewis said by way of greeting. When I shook his hand, it was gnarled and solid, with numerous scars making miniature maps.

"Bourbon?" Sonny was already holding a different bottle.

Lewis nodded. "Sonny tells me you folks is interested in that fella I pulled outta the water a few months ago."

"That's right," I said.

"Well, we was coming back in, saw something bobbing in the waves. Got the gaff and brought her in. Realized it were a body."

"What did you do?"

"Pulled it up on deck, while Yanto called the cops."

"Any I.D. on him?"

"Didn't find a wallet, nothin' else to say who he was. Later they said he were some kinda artist fella."

"Tell us about the body."

"Had all his clothes on, 'cept one shoe was missing. Looked like he'd been banged up pretty bad, though. Musta got hammered against the rocks a bit, then washed back out."

"So his face was all battered?"

"Face and head." Lewis shrugged. "Couldn't tell about the rest of him, 'cause like I say, he were dressed."

"Did it look like he drowned?"

"Mighta."

I raised my eyebrows.

Lewis shrugged. "I've seen drowned folks. I wouldna said it. But later on, they said he did."

"They might have got that wrong. Any other marks?"

"I didn't check him stem to stern, you know. He was dead. Left him stretched out on the deck until they came to get him."

"What do you guess? He fell off a boat?"

"He warn't really dressed for being out on the water. No one come for'ard to say he'd been on their boat, though, and no small craft were reported missing."

I spread my hands. "If he didn't fall off a boat, how'd he get out there?"

Lewis shrugged. "Maybe out walking along the rocks by the shore and got taken by a wave. Happens from time to time."

"What did the police say?"

"Like I said. Just an accident, and he drowned."

I chewed my lip, unable to come up with anything important to ask. Lewis drained the last of his bourbon and set the glass down. "Anything else?"

Something bothered me about the account, but I couldn't put words to it. "I guess not. Thank you."

"Now it's time to get me some lunch."

"Enjoy your lobster," I said.

"Lobster!" Lewis almost spat. "I haul them goddamned things up every day. I'm sick of 'em. I'm getting some of them hot dogs." We all laughed. He nodded and left.

Allison held out her empty wine glass to Sonny. "Think I could get a refill?" He smiled and complied.

She turned to me. "I'm going to need this, because I know that look on your face."

"What look?" I tried to appear innocent.

"That 'I've got a mystery' look. You like to play Hardy Boys, and now you've got this mysterious death to investigate."

Sonny eyed me. "What is it you do again?"

"Security consultant, right now," I said. "But I'm looking for someone. He was tied in to the art colony where this drowned guy came from. Maybe there's a connection."

"But you're not a private eye," Sonny said. "I can see why. Didn't seem like you got much information."

I shrugged. "It never does. One little piece at a time, like a jigsaw puzzle. Next I want to talk to that Mrs. Perkins, who runs the art colony down near Ogunquit." I looked at J.C.

"You know her, don't you? Can you introduce us, so I can talk to her without her bodyguard jumping me?"

"No."

"Sorry, what?"

"No, I'm not going to do it. The last time I got someone to help you, he got in trouble and lost his job."

I looked at him in disbelief. "Well, I'm sorry about that, but I made it right, didn't I?"

"With him. Not with me. I lost a good contact. I won't do that again." He was dead serious.

"But you brought us today."

"Sonny can handle himself, as can Lewis. But you have a way of attracting serious problems, and I don't want to expose vulnerable people to that."

I felt embarrassed and hurt, and left in a huff. J.C. was my friend, so what was all this shit about? I went out and sat by the water. Dark thoughts and ideas rattled in my head like a rock in my shoe. Allison had called it. I'd stumbled on a mystery, and it was nagging at me. All I'd wanted to do was find some kid who hadn't talked with his grandmother in a while, and I'd uncovered thugs, liars, an art war, and maybe a murder. All kinds of things scuttle out when you turn over enough rocks.

I looked out to sea, at the wide expanse of water surrounding this tiny jewel of Casco Bay. On another island, not far from this one, I'd encountered an old Yakuza boss who messed up my life and almost got me killed. And things had been worse on the mainland, more death and loss. Though I loved my new home, and found it a healing place, I kept running into trouble.

Sonny came over a few minutes later. "You're one hell of a guest."

"Sorry."

"Well, if you can't have any fun on a day like this, that's your problem."

"J.C. surprised me, turning on me like that."

"Got your panties in a twist, do ya?"

I said nothing, getting even more steamed.

"Why you want to talk to Lottie Perkins?"

I looked up. "We've got one dead artist, another one missing, a third who runs from questions and calls the goon squad on me. All were connected to her colony. Something's going on, and I need to know more."

"J.C. says that biker fella who wants to kill you is still out there somewhere. Would Lottie be in any danger if she talked to you? She's a good woman. I don't want to send any more trouble her way."

"Sounds like she's already got some trouble. She's got a bodyguard. I can't see how asking questions would be a problem."

Sonny laughed. "It ain't the questions. It's how you go tearing off after you hear the answers. You'll go and stir the shit up."

"Everybody seems to think so."

"Lottie's been bothered for some time, though. Maybe you could do something about that."

I gave him a steady gaze. "I can't promise anything. But I won't deliberately put her in any danger."

"You better not," said Sonny. "Or I'll kill you myself."

Dale T. Phillips

CHAPTER 11

When Allison and I got home from the clambake, we took a walk along Promenade Way. As the sun set, I looked out to the ocean, back toward Peak's Island.

"I had a nice time," said Allison. "Sonny is a stitch."

"And he seems quite taken with you."

"Think he'd treat me better than you do?"

"A fisherman's life is even more dangerous than mine. You'd hate it."

"Why can't I settle down with a nice, boring accountant?"

"Because you wild girls always go for the bad boys."

She punched me in the shoulder, but laughed. We walked for a bit more.

"Maybe you're right," she said. "Maybe it is the darkness that makes you attractive. I know you've tried to step away from the violence, but you'll never change."

"I'm sorry," I said, and meant it.

"Yeah, me too. Guess I have to accept you as you are."

"Some of that's good."

"Some of it is," she agreed, and kissed me. The kissing got a little intense, and she spoke to me in a husky voice. "Let's get back home."

We did, in record time. We started kissing again as soon as we got the front door closed, and tried to undress each other as we moved toward the bedroom. Good thing there was no one else at home, because we didn't make it all the way. There was urgency in our need, a pent-up energy.

After a time, we got up from the floor, picked up what clothes we could find, all flushed like hormonal teenagers, and finally got to the bedroom.

She went off to the shower. I soon joined her. We took a long, loving soak under the spray, taking turns lathering each other up and rinsing off. It got us going again, and we ended the shower, toweled off, and got in the big, insanely comfy, four-poster bed. Then we took our time.

Now we were slowly getting in sync with each other, feeling our heartbeats sing a loving tune. We kissed and caressed without hurry, making sure we savored every feeling. After a long, long time, she took the lead, riding atop me and moving to an ancient rhythm. Her eyes were closed as she moved back and forth, and I looked up and marveled that this wonderful, desirable woman would love me so. I touched her, feeling the heat from her flesh, stroking her, wrapping my fingers in her hair.

Afterward, we lay in each other's arms, thoroughly spent and immeasurably pleased with ourselves. We made small talk, nibbling an ear or shoulder every now and then, clasping hands, tracing circles on skin. After a time she fell asleep.

I lay there thinking of art wars and criminals.

The next morning, I picked up the phone when it rang.

The voice on the other end was old but still strong. "May I speak with Zachary Taylor, please?"

"That's me."

"Mr. Taylor, this is Loretta Perkins. Sonny called me and said it was important that you speak with me. I understand you are the man who caused such a ruckus at my colony."

"Yes, ma'am, sorry about that, but I was attacked, and I hadn't done anything."

Her voice was frosty. "You were trespassing."

"It was my understanding that the public was allowed on the grounds."

"Welcome visitors, yes."

"Would you tell me what I did to make me unwelcome?"

Her voice was the vocal whip-crack of a stern librarian. "You had been snooping around."

"If you mean asking questions, yes, I was."

"And why were you doing that?"

"Because a lovely woman is dying down in Florida, and she wanted to see her grandson Steven one last time. I went to the gallery where he worked, and your buddy Mr. Abernathy got all squirrelly, like he had something to hide."

There was a pause. "We have nothing to hide."

"If that's so, you should talk to me, and we can settle this, and I can go away. I can give you the number for the attorney of Steven's grandmother, so you can verify I'm telling the truth."

Another pause. "All right."

I read off the number from Saul's card, and she told me she'd call me back.

I did some stretching exercises until the phone rang.

The crisp voice came over the line again. "Well, it appears that your story checks out."

"So you'll talk to me?"

"I suppose you'll continue to snoop around until I say yes."

She kept needling me, but she wasn't the only one who could play that game. "Did Mr. Rabinowitz tell you she doesn't have much time left?"

"Stop trying to make me feel guilty. If it will buy me some peace, then yes, I'll speak with you."

"Where should I meet you?"

"You'd better come here." Of course. She'd want home court advantage. She recited directions, and I told her I'd be there as soon as I could. I doubted she'd be baking me cookies.

Mrs. Perkins was old Maine money, and the size of the estate reflected that fact. The property was enormous, and I had to pass through a massive gate anchored by stone walls just to get on the grounds. Then it was a long driveway and another gate, with a closed-circuit camera pointed at me. Here stone surrounded the inner sanctum like medieval castle walls, shutting out the unwelcome world, as if there were still barbarian invaders. Maybe to her it seemed that way.

I pulled up to the second gate, and a voice squawked at me from the intercom box. I gave them my name, and the metal barrier swung open enough to let me through. I drove down the long stretch of driveway and saw the manse. It was impressive, if one liked the idea of blowing a few million bucks to impress the hell out of people with scale. It was more like a small town than a home, with outbuildings scattered abundantly, though all dwarfed by the central building itself.

Before the main house was a huge circular drive big enough to land a plane on. I parked out in front with my beater car, a huge, ugly, green Chevy. Let them look at that for a while. Maybe it would give them the vapors.

I've got nothing against money, but just didn't think it conferred any special anointing of superiority. Since this place would have sufficed for a landed baroness, it appeared a mite ostentatious. Even if it was the family estate.

I went to the wide double-doors and rang. They'd probably have preferred I go around back to the servant's entrance, but here I was.

An older man in a suit answered. I was relieved to see it wasn't the bodyguard.

I smiled at him. "Zack Taylor to see Mrs. Perkins."

He nodded. "Please follow me."

Inside, it looked like the old movies of European palace interiors. Paintings, sculptures, decorations, all tried to fill the massive space, as if the inhabitants were afraid of seeing too much emptiness. We walked across polished marble, and my guide opened a door and announced me. I stepped through into a library, filled floor-to-ceiling with shelves of leather-bound volumes. My guide discreetly retired, pulling the doors closed behind him.

Mrs. Perkins was a white-haired lady who dressed well, and of course, expensively. She sat in an elaborately carved chair and didn't get up when I came in. Behind her on the wall was a huge, full-length painting of a woman in a gown, who was staring down at me. They looked me over like I was a muddy muskrat that had traipsed across the elegant rug. "Let's get this over with," the woman sighed.

Great to see you too, lady.

"Nice library. I don't see your gorilla. So is Professor Plum coming after me with a candlestick?"

She gave me the fisheye, cocking her head to the side. "What on earth are you talking about?"

"The board game, Clue?"

She stared at me. She hadn't one.

"Never mind," I said. "So Abernathy works for you?"

The question took her by surprise, as it was meant to. She sputtered for a bit in answering. "We have mutual interests. He advises me on artistic endeavors."

"Like having people assaulted at his say-so?"

"As I told you before, you were snooping."

"And as I told you, all I did was show up at his gallery and ask about Steven. He lied and acted like I'd uncovered a dirty little secret. Then the next time he sees me, he freaks out and sics your guard dog on me. And why do you have a bodyguard like that in the first place? When a few simple questions cause such a disruption, it's obvious there's something going on."

The woman had been rapidly blinking as I made my speech. She reached out a hand to touch the table, and burst into tears. Well, that was something I hadn't expected.

"Are you all right?"

"Who are you?" She sobbed. "Who do you work for?"

"You spoke to Mr. Rabinowitz, so you know the answer. I'm working for a woman who wants to see her grandson. Is there something going on with him?"

"Are you in any way connected with the Holloways?"

"Your arch-enemies? No."

She stared at me, as if examining me for a lie.

"Look," I said. "I know Sonny, and I also know J.C. Reed. He can vouch for me, though he thought it might upset you if he asked you to talk to me."

"Well, it certainly looks as if he was right." She managed a weak smile, and I liked her for it.

"I don't know what's going on, and I don't know the Holloways. I understand you're having some problems with them."

"They are criminals. They pose as art dealers, but they are no better than common street thugs. Have you ever heard of the Kray brothers?"

I bobbled the name around my memory for a minute. "Yeah, they were twins in the London crime scene back a few decades."

"The Holloways are our Krays, and just as ruthless."

"Twins, huh?"

"Identical. You never know which one you're talking to. They make a game of it." She dabbed at her eyes with a silk handkerchief she'd produced from her sleeve.

"So what's their racket?"

"Anything and everything, legal or not. Cheating buyers with underhanded dealing, fraud, coercion, blackmail, outright thievery, you name it, they've done it. They're trying to corner the art market here in Maine, but they don't want to stop at that. There's only one thing holding them back."

"What's that?"

"Me."

I ran it through in my head. "You're at war with them, and you thought I was working with them. And yet you didn't have your bodyguard here."

"Here, you're my guest. But I still didn't know for certain. You showed up and started snooping around. They've had others do similar things."

"Well that explains my reception at your art colony."

"That's the one thing I've managed to keep out of their hands until now."

I nodded, understanding why she was paranoid. "How did this all get started?"

"Some years back, they appeared and began to buy up galleries, art, and even the artists themselves. They got everything cheap back then, and since the value of much of it has gone up immensely, they're worth millions. What they couldn't get legally, they cheated or had someone steal it for them. Nothing that could be proven, of course, but their hand was on every dirty deal. They grew in power and influence, crushed everything and everyone in their path, and now I'm the only thing that stands between them and their dominating the entire art community here in southern Maine."

"So what's it all about, then?"

She sighed. "For them, money, plain and simple. When they control it all, there are enormous sums to be made. They seem not to care about anything else. It has cost me dearly to fight them, but it's worth it."

"Steven was at your colony. What happened?"

"Steven is a very talented young man, so of course we persuaded him to take a fellowship with us. Regrettably, he formed an attachment to another artist."

"Bosco."

She cocked her head to peer at me. "You have done a bit of snooping."

"And Bosco was causing trouble?"

"Along with his obvious artistic talent, Bosco has a talent for mischief as well. As an artist, he indulges in unsavory practices."

"Like heroin?"

The flesh on her face sagged. "Yes. We even offered to help him, but he refused. We simply cannot have that kind of thing at our retreat, so he was asked to leave. Steven as well, regrettably."

"So what happened with your other mishap? Another one of your artists was found dead in the water."

She put a hand to her brow. "Poor Owen. With all the other things going on, and then that."

"What do you think happened?"

She stared at me. "The police said he drowned."

I shrugged. "Maybe. Could it be something else?"

Her eyes went wide. "Whatever do you mean?"

"You're having a war. Maybe the Holloways decided to up the stakes."

Her gaze darted from side to side. "I do not want to believe that."

"If there's that much money at stake, we shouldn't rule it out. Was Owen involved in anything? The heroin, maybe?"

"No, Owen was a model of behavior. Completely upright, almost to a fault." She put her hand back to her head. "It pains me to talk about this."

"Well, I'm sorry about that. All I did was ask a few questions, and now I find out a war is going on."

"It was not of my making. It was those awful men."

"I'm going to keep asking questions until I find out the truth. That's what I'm good at."

She sighed. "I could pay you to stop messing about."

I smiled. "No, you couldn't. This is personal, a favor to a woman who hasn't got much time left. On the other hand, you help me find Steven, and I'm out of your hair."

"I'm afraid I don't know where he is."

"He was at your art colony, and he worked in the gallery run by your friend."

"We assumed he ran off with that awful St. Clair."

"They were that close?"

"Steven was rather distraught when St. Clair was told to never set foot on our grounds again. It became clear that he had to leave as well."

"What did he say?"

"I don't know. I was not there when he departed. It was upsetting. He's quite talented."

"So he left a rather nice, safe position to run off with an addict lover?"

"Oh, you make it all sound so lurid."

"It doesn't sound like a smart move. I can't imagine openings like that are easy to come by, and living with someone on an expensive habit gets you into trouble fast."

"I hope he's all right."

"Well, I'll find out as soon as I can." I thought it over. "You don't suppose the Holloways offered him a better deal?"

She looked up. "What do you mean?"

"If you're at war, wouldn't it be a win for them to hire Steven away from under your wing? Especially since he also worked at one of your galleries? Sounds like they might enjoy using him as a pawn in the game against you."

"I had some discreet inquiries made. He has not been seen since he left us."

"Inquiries? By whom?"

"A private investigator."

"You had a PI looking around? It would help me a great deal to talk to him."

"It's her, actually. But she found no trace of Steven." She considered this for a bit. "I suppose it's for the best." She got up and went over to a massive rolltop desk. She took out a piece of paper and uncapped a fountain pen. She wrote something, recapped the pen, and walked over to give me the paper. "Here is her name and address."

"I'm curious. How did you find someone to do this kind of work? Yellow pages?"

"Mr. Abernathy recommended her."

"I see. Please don't call her, or Mr. Abernathy, to tell them I'm coming."

"Don't you want that, so she'll talk to you?"

"Not at first. I like to see what reception I get when I surprise someone. I'll have her call you when we talk, so I can watch her reaction as well. Will she be able to reach you here?"

"Yes, or my secretary will know where to reach me."

"Thank you, Mrs. Perkins. This is a big help. I'm sorry we got off on the wrong foot."

"We certainly did."

"What would Isabella think of all this?" I raised my eyes to the woman in the painting, Isabella Stewart Gardner. I'd figured it out.

"She'd have enjoyed it. I met her, you know."

"What was she like?"

"Elegant, gracious, astonishing. I was only a child then. It was 1918, before her first stroke. But I wanted to grow up and be like her."

"And surround yourself with art?"

"And cause a stir wherever I went." For just a minute, I saw a twinkle of a lively past in the eyes of this woman. I'll bet she had some great stories to tell. But it was evident she wanted me gone, so I obliged her. I certainly liked her a lot more than I had at the start of our meeting.

CHAPTER 12

Private Investigator Dolores King had a downtown, ground-floor office, just off Congress Street. There was no response when I rang the bell, so I went across the street and hung out on a bench, after buying a *Press Herald* from a vending machine. Since I'd stopped off to change into my suit, I hoped I looked like a thoroughly respectable loiterer.

Hours went by. I'd get up and walk around every so often, then go back to my spot. My stomach was grumbling, reminding me of the stretch of time since I'd last fed it, and was insisting I give up the stakeout. I tried to ignore it, and read the paper all the way through for the ninth time.

Finally, a blond woman in jeans went to the street door, unlocked it, and went inside. I gave her another two minutes, then went in myself. There was a tiny reception area and an inner office. The door to the office was open, so I could see her seated behind a desk. She looked to be in her forties, and not the early part. The woman looked up, and her hand shot to her purse on the desk next to her. I thought I looked respectable enough, but maybe I was giving off a bad vibe.

"Easy," I said. "I'm here on business, so you don't need whatever you were reaching for."

Her brows scrunched together, as if she was annoyed. Deep face lines made it seem like she did this a lot. Her eyes and the downturned creases at the corners of her mouth told me she'd seen too many hard truths, and didn't like most of them.

"I was just getting my cigarettes. What do you want?" Her voice was hard-edged as well, so she was probably a long-time smoker.

I went into her office. "Is that how you greet all your prospective clients?"

She snorted, and her eyes remained narrowed. "You're not a client. What do you want?"

"May I sit?"

She waved a hand at the chair on my side, and took out a pack of cigarettes. That wasn't what she'd been reaching for when she spied me, but she was covering. She snapped a lighter and ignited her cancer stick. She clicked the lighter shut and dragged deeply before she blew out a plume of smoke. She was overplaying the tough-cookie, private eye role, and I hoped she wouldn't take out a bottle of whiskey.

The business had given us time to assess each other. Her reactions had told me she was jumpy about something, and I liked that, because it gave me leverage. People who got unduly nervous before the talk even started usually had something to hide.

"I need your help finding someone," I said. "They seem to have gone off the grid, and I'm told you can help locate them."

"Bullshit."

"Steven Harris. That name ring a bell?"

She started, and the cigarette almost fell out. Her eyes narrowed further, to little more than slits, and combined with a slight curl to her lip, I was reminded of an animal that sensed danger and was ready to fight back.

"Who sent you?" It came out harsh.

"Loretta Perkins, your client," I said. "When she found out I was looking for Steven, she told me she'd retained you for that purpose."

"Why are you looking for him?"

"His grandmother in Florida is dying, and wants to see him."

"I'm afraid I don't know where he is. I was unsuccessful." She looked away and gave a nervous little flick of her cigarette toward an ashtray.

"So I heard. Can you tell me what you did to locate him, so I don't have to waste time and effort?"

"That's confidential. Client privilege."

"Mrs. Perkins said for you to call her to okay it. She wants you to cooperate with me fully. Why don't you give her a call?"

"I don't share information like that. Policy." She stubbed out her cigarette with some force, as if it was my head she was grinding into the ashtray.

"Ah, then maybe you can just give me a hint of where you looked, what steps you took, that kind of thing."

She stared at me like I was something that had crawled into her house that she didn't know how to get rid of. "Who are you, anyway?"

"Zack Taylor."

"You look a little familiar. But you're not a cop. And you're not a PI from here."

"Just doing a favor for a friend. It sounded like an easy task. But is there some mystery to Steven's disappearance?"

She shrugged. "Not that I know of."

"Is he trying to avoid being located?"

"I didn't get a sense of that."

"Did you talk to Bosco?"

She blinked rapidly and licked her lips while she thought of which lie to tell. "Yes, but he didn't know where Steven is, either."

"Hmm. And how did you get in touch with Bosco?"

Her eyes shifted from side to side. "I think somebody told me where he'd be one night. A bar."

"Who was that helpful person?"

"Confidential." She eyed the cigarette pack.

"Who else did you talk to?"

"That's confidential, too."

"As is your whole 'investigation,' apparently. Well, you sure put the 'con' in confidential."

Her mouth was pinched together. "You got something to say about how I do business?"

"Yes, I do." I leaned forward and put my elbows on her desk, encroaching on her space. It was time for a hard shake of the tree. "Mrs. Perkins paid you money to do a job, and yet you won't say a damn thing about it, or cooperate in any way, even though she wants it. So either you lied about even trying to find him, or you're holding something back you shouldn't. Either way, you're in big trouble."

"How do you figure?" She gripped the metal lighter like it was a weapon. "Maybe I just don't want to talk to you. I don't even know you."

"Will you talk to Mrs. Perkins? Tell her what, if anything, you did?"

"The case is closed. He flew the coop."

"Not even close. It's just started, and you're in the hot seat. If you took money from her and didn't do the job, you committed fraud. That alone should be good for getting your PI license yanked. And I'm connected to Lieutenant McClaren of the Portland PD. Maybe you've heard of him. I'll bet he'll have some questions for you." I didn't tell her that McClaren thought I was a major thorn in his side, but I liked dropping his name and seeing her flinch again.

"I didn't do anything wrong."

"So why so skittish over a simple request? I don't know what someone told you or offered you, but you're in deeper than you thought. I'm proof of that, and I'm not going away, unless you tell me what you know of Steven and Bosco. You've got a chance to make things right before it all goes south, but when this blows open, you're going into the wood-chipper. Spin it how you want, but there are other people who are going to find out just how deep you're in. Accessory and conspiracy for starters, I'll wager. Maybe this got out of hand, and there's kidnapping or murder involved. You ready for fifteen-to-life?"

She slammed the lighter down on the desk, making a sharp crack. "Look, asshole, I don't know who you are or what your game is. You come in here making threats, but you better watch your step."

"Or what?" I smiled. "You going to rough me up?"

"I know some people that can."

"I'd like to meet them. Are they connected to this case, too? Then I can ask them what they know."

"You won't be asking anything when they get done with you. Now get out."

I rose and left, closing the door behind me. I waited about a half-minute, and poked my head back in. She had another cigarette lit, and was speaking into the telephone. She looked like she'd been caught with her hand in the cookie jar.

"Say hi to your thug friends for me," I said. "I'm looking forward to our conversation."

Dale T. Phillips

CHAPTER 13

After grabbing some lunch to take care of my growling stomach, I called Mrs. Perkins and told her about Dolores King. I suggested she ask her good friend Mr. Abernathy why he'd recommended a PI who hadn't done what she was hired to do. Abernathy would come up with some excuse, but I wanted to turn the heat on. And I'd start following him to see what he might be up to, but I also wanted to tail Dolores and see where she might run. But as a PI, she'd have a better sense of a tail than most people, so I'd have to be careful.

I had convinced Mrs. Perkins to allow me back on the grounds of the colony, so I could get more insight as to the artists and their relationships. I questioned her as how best to approach the Holloway twins, and she told me they were having one of their gallery shows that night in Portland. I decided to make an appearance.

A few hours later, I entered a chic little gallery on the edge of the Old Port district. There were several rooms. And quite a few people. I scanned the crowd, and saw a tall black man across the room, his head above the rest. Theo. I'd met Thelonius M. Burbee on the set of the movie I'd been a consultant for, and cost him his job when the movie backer got killed and the filming was suddenly canceled.

I started to make my way through the crowd to get to him, but was interrupted by Mason Carter, a jerk reporter I'd tangled with on a few occasions.

He held a plastic cup of what looked to be white wine. "What the hell are you doing here?"

"It's a gallery show, dipshit," I replied. "I'm here to see some art."

"Bullshit. You don't follow art."

"Oh, but I do. Just because you can't tell a Picasso from a Rembrandt doesn't mean others are as ignorant."

"You still owe me for the camera you broke," he said.

"You keep getting in my face, and I'll break more than that. The last time I saw you, you were being taken away in handcuffs. Want to try for an ambulance?"

"You wouldn't dare. Maybe I'll spill this wine on you, see if you'll punch me in front of all these people."

"And maybe that large security guard coming our way will hoist you by your collar and pitch you out of here. Want to find out?"

Carter looked back over his shoulder and saw Theo approach. Even with a smiling face, Theo looked scary to most people, huge and menacing. Carter made a face and skittered off into the crowd.

"Thanks," I said, when Theo got near. "I might have bopped him one."

"I'd say it's good to see you, but I know better," said Theo. "You here to cause trouble?"

"Actually, I am. What do you know about the Holloways?"

"The guys running this shindig? They pay well. You gonna fuck this job up for me, too?" But he smiled when he said it.

"I hope not. Tell you what. If they sic you on me, I'll take a dive, make it look good while you throw me out."

Theo smiled. "A dive? Implying it might come out another way, were you to protest your expulsion?"

Theo had played football for LSU, and still looked to be in great shape. He was easily twice my size, and could likely wrap me up like a pretzel, being the proverbial guy you didn't want to meet in a dark alley.

"Well, I wouldn't want to bleed all over your nice suit. Better than a uniform, huh?"

"That's for sure. Two women have given me their number tonight. Said they might need some security work."

"Is that what they're calling it, now?"

"Long as they pay," he said.

"Gigolo sideline to augment the security guard pay," I said. "Nice to see you branching out."

Theo looked at his watch. "So how long before I get called to throw you out of here?"

"A few minutes, anyway. I've never met the Holloways, so I don't know how it's going to go. What do they look like?"

"Like a couple of wolves eyeing a flock of sheep. You'll know them when you see them. Those guys give me the creeps. You watch yourself. What did they do to you, anyway?"

"Nothing yet. But the night is young. Wish me luck."

"Just don't bust up any of the artwork. It costs more than you're worth."

He moved away to stand against a wall, scanning the crowd. I looked around for the Holloways, and realized Theo had been right. I saw one man surrounded by a knot of people, holding court. While they all looked like they belonged in a gallery, he could have played the suave supervillain in an action film. He was tall, with a pronounced widow's peak in his hair, and dressed expensively. I looked around, and saw his twin studying a painting on one wall, with a shorter man beside him. I went on over and stood just beyond the range of his peripheral vision. Predators are sensitive to being stalked, and this one was no exception. He swiveled his head to look at me, as if I'd spoken to him. He excused himself to the other man, and came over to me. I watched him approach, and wondered how soon it would be before the twin telepathy brought the second brother over. I looked for the other one, and here he came. In a moment, both brothers stood before me, two sharks repelling another who had encroached on their territory.

"Let me guess," said one. "You're the guy causing all the trouble."

"What trouble is that?"

The second one piped up. "Well, getting Loretta Perkins to throw you out of her elitist art colony, for one thing."

I smiled. "All a misunderstanding."

"Of course it is," said the first. I realized they did this deliberately, to keep a person bouncing their attention back and forth between them.

"So what do I call you two to tell you apart? Thing One and Thing Two?"

"I'm Preston, and he's Canby. What was your name again?" The one identified as Preston leaned in.

I snapped up a business card, practically in his face. He recoiled, and then reached out to take it, giving his brother a look.

"Zack Taylor, Security Consultant," said Canby, reading over his brother's shoulder. "Interesting."

"What kind of security do you do?" Preston looked up at me.

I smiled. "Just about anything that's legal and pays."

They exchanged another glance, and Canby nodded slightly. "It just so happens we have a need for someone with your talents. Do you have a passport?"

"I do."

"Our associates in England have need of a man like you. Say three months' work? And we could pay you well." He named a figure that almost made me whistle. I could have bought a couple of new cars with that much.

Instead, I laughed. "That is the quickest and slickest attempt at a bribe I've ever heard."

"I assure you, we're quite sincere."

"If it's worth that much to you to get me out of your hair for a time, I must be on to something."

They realized I wasn't dumb or greedy, so they switched gears. "We deal in delicate negotiations for a lot of money. Someone like you bouncing around makes buyers nervous. We don't want to lose a sale."

"Then just tell me where I can find Steven, and I'll go away."

"Ah, yes," said one. "Loretta's pet, from the colony. Seems her patronage wasn't all it was cracked up to be."

"Do you know his whereabouts?"

"Afraid not."

"Then I'll just have to keep poking around."

"That might not be healthy." Canby had a dangerous level of menace in his voice.

I laughed again. "Oh, I've already been threatened, thanks. By that useless lady PI that Abernathy hired for Mrs. Perkins. I don't suppose she's an associate of yours?"

"We don't know who you're talking about. We do know Abernathy, of course. Perkins' lapdog."

"So why would he not be interested in helping find this guy, if she wanted him found?"

Preston shrugged. It seemed an elegant gesture, almost French. "Can't tell you."

I looked from one to the other, and the lightbulb went on. "If he's dicking her around, you guys would know about it. And you'd use it. So he's working for you, playing both sides of the fence. Wow."

They exchanged another glance. Now Canby had a crease across his brow. "You really don't want to be messing in our business."

"What's that? Having a war with Mrs. Perkins?"

"The old biddy thinks she's the reincarnation of Isabella Stewart Gardner. The last protector of pure art against the ravages of the Philistines. We're businessmen. We make a lot of money in this world. You have the potential to disrupt business, and we won't stand for that. What's it going to take for you to go away?"

"I told you. Produce Steven, or point me to where he is."

"And we told you, we don't know."

"Then gentlemen, we have a problem."

"You have one, that's for certain," muttered Preston, and they both turned away. When they did, I saw the way the backs of their suits were cut. Each had a gun back there, in a belt holster, very discreet, very hard to detect, unless you knew what to look for.

I knew I'd made two very bad enemies.

CHAPTER 14

When leaving the gallery the night before, I'd slipped one of my business cards to Theo and told him to call me in the morning. At nine the phone rang.

"Thanks for not causing a ruckus last night," Theo's rumbling voice came over the line. "After you left, they both looked like they'd eaten lemons. Not happy at all."

"Yeah, they tried to bribe me, then threatened me. I noticed they were packing. What kind of art gallery owners carry guns?"

"The wrong kind." He was actually chuckling, though I didn't see anything amusing.

"I think they're going to make some kind of move against me. They kind of have to. So if my body turns up, point the cops in the right direction."

"Which one? You got enemies on all sides."

"Funny guy. Is that any way to talk to your new boss?"

"Say that again?"

"I'm offering you some work. Want it?"

"Yeah, last night was a one-off. Schedule's clear, unfortunately. What you got in mind?"

"Just a shadow job. Surveillance and maybe tailing. I can't do it, because I've got someone else to follow."

His laughter boomed. "You want me? The most easily-spotted black shadow in all Portland?"

"I do. She's a lady PI, and she'd likely spot whoever followed her. So I'll make damn sure she knows she's got a tail, and we're not even hiding it. I want her nervous as hell."

Theo paused. "She gonna shoot at me?"

"Hope not, though she packs a purse gun. You licensed, just in case?"

"Yup. Guess I better bring it along."

"Right. If she comes after you, by all means, get the hell out. But I think you'll scare the crap out of her. She's tied in with some big stuff, and won't want any attention. I'm squeezing things, which means she may try to run. Don't break any laws catching her. If she loses you, oh well."

"Wait a minute. Lady PI? What's her name?"

"Dolores King."

"That's it." He snapped his thick fingers. "She carries a Donna Karan purse, because it's got her initials. Worked with her on a job a couple years ago. Not a nice person."

"Gotta tell you Theo, she says she knows some very bad guys. So be real careful about who's behind you, in case she calls someone. Anything doesn't smell right, any bad vibes, you get the hell out. You'll get hazard pay, but getting hurt is not part of the deal. I want her rattled, but I don't want her sending the dogs after you."

"You'll be drawing them all to yourself, won't you?"

"That's the plan."

"Thought so. That's pretty stupid, you know."

"Thanks. I want you calling her office every hour or so, too. I want her jumping every time the phone rings."

"Okay, when do I start, and where do I go?"

I gave him the address of her office and the phone number, and told him I'd meet him there in thirty minutes.

A short time later, I went downtown and saw him in his car at a metered parking space where he could watch the door.

"Hello, Mr. Unobtrusive."

He spread his hands. "You asked for it."

"The police know you, or are you going to get hassled?"

"I know a few of them. Some work as off-duty security. Anyone rousts me, I can give them a name or two to call."

"Good." I passed him an envelope with a few hundred-dollar bills inside. "First couple days' worth."

He looked inside, and smiled. "Shit, you do feel guilty about getting the film job shut down."

"Just remember, hospital bills and bullet holes in your car aren't covered."

"And no dental plan?"

"Hell, no. You're migrant help. I can always find another two-hundred-forty pound, black ex-linebacker to fill in if you don't work out."

"In Portland? Who you calling? Thugs 'R Us?"

"Just keep your eyes open. Don't want you getting hurt."

Dale T. Phillips

CHAPTER 15

I was getting set to drive down to Ogunquit and start shadowing Abernathy when I got the phone call.

"Zack? It's me, Peggy."

"Yeah, how you doing?"

"I need to see you, but I don't want to leave the colony grounds. I was attacked."

"What? Are you all right?"

"I guess. Mostly shaken up. I'm scared. How can I see you?"

"I had a talk with Mrs. Perkins. They'll let me on the grounds now. I'll be there in a few minutes."

I drove way too fast getting to the colony. When I went into the welcome house and saw Peggy, she looked pale, and her eyes were red. The woman who had been with her excused herself and left us alone.

"Tell me what happened."

"I went to Portland to do some grocery shopping. I came out of Shop 'n Save with my bags, and someone grabbed me from behind in the parking lot. There were two of them. They were the ones we saw that night in the alley outside the bar. They didn't even try to hide their faces. The big one held me while the other grabbed my face and warned me."

"What did he say?"

"'You and your boyfriend stuck your noses in where they don't belong, bitch, but you better not do it again. Either of you. Stay in your little cabin and paint, or we'll be back, and you might never paint again. And tell that guy if we see him again, it'll be the last time anyone does.'" Her eyes looked haunted. "Then he showed me a gun."

"Then what?"

"The asshole who was holding me groped me and whispered in my ear that maybe they'd have some fun with me first. The other one said I'd really hate that, wouldn't I? Then they laughed and the one holding me pushed me down. I'd been terrified, but now I was fucking pissed off. I saw the one who'd grabbed me. He had a bandage over his nose, and two black eyes. They got in their car and drove away, but I got their plate number. Here it is." She handed me a slip of paper.

"Do you want to talk to the police?"

"Hell, no. Won't do me any good if they catch these guys after I'm dead. I have a feeling you can keep that from happening."

I nodded approval. "Peggy, you did great. Most people would have been too shaken up to do anything but cry. I'm so sorry this happened. It's okay if they come after me, but I didn't expect them to go for you. They must have found out who you were from the night we talked to Bosco. That means they're really wired in to this place. I think Abernathy works for the Holloways, and Mrs. Perkins doesn't know it yet. So you watch out for him if he comes back here. I'm going to shadow that little asshole, but first I'm going to take care of these guys."

"Don't get killed on my account."

"I won't, but they won't be using those hands for some time."

She smiled. "I'd like that. But tell you the truth, they scared the shit out of me."

"They were supposed to. Maybe it's better for you to stay here until I take care of this." I thought it over. "I've got an even better idea. Do you have any empty cabins here?"

"Yeah, we've always got a spare or two."

"How about if I get a guy to come here, just to keep an eye on things? He's big and scary-looking, and while he's here, you'll be perfectly safe."

I could see the relief in her eyes. "Don't go to any trouble."

"No trouble. I'll call Mrs. Perkins and clear it. Let me use your phone."

I dialed Theo's pager number. While I waited for him to call back, I dialed Mrs. Perkins and told her that after meeting the Holloways, I was arranging extra protection, with an on-site security guard. She approved, and even offered to pay for it. I guess she'd forgiven me for our first encounter, or else subscribed to the belief "the enemy of my enemy is my friend."

Theo rang me back. "No sign of her yet," he said.

"Change of plans, Theo. They went after somebody not involved, threatened her and roughed her up, so I'm going to ask you to bodyguard her for a couple of days. Here on site twenty-four seven, make sure they stay away. You good with that?"

"You're paying. Guess it'd be better than sitting in the car. I'd have to swing by my place, pick up my go bag."

"That's fine, I'll stay until you get here. Any of your cop contacts able to run a plate for you?" The last time I'd had someone run a plate number for me, he'd lost his job. So I felt guilty, but I needed to let these goons know if they threatened other people, there was going to be blowback.

"Yeah, I know a guy."

"Okay, here it is." I read him the number on the paper.

Theo arrived an hour later, and I made introductions. Peggy agreed to arrange his sleeping quarters and introduce him to the others. She looked far less stressed, and I felt I'd done the right thing, for once.

Theo also had the name and address that matched the car's registration. With the colony now secured, I was off to do some damage.

CHAPTER 16

The car driven by the thugs that had attacked Peggy was registered to a Dwight Pierce, with an address on the north side of Portland. I drove back to town and found the place, and saw the car on the street, a black Cadillac. I parked nearby and walked back. Taking out my Swiss Army knife, I spiked the two tires closest to the curb. Then I went to the gas station next door and stayed out of sight.

About twenty minutes later, a guy came out and walked to the Cadillac. I recognized him from the alley outside Bosco's bar, the one who'd pointed his gun at me.

His voice carried all the way over to me. "What the fuck?" He knelt down for a closer look. I slipped up behind him as he stood back up.

"Man, that's some bad karma," I said.

He whirled, and his eyes went wide as his hand shot inside his jacket for the gun. I dropped to one knee and drove my right fist into his crotch. I stood up as he went down, clutching himself. His mouth was open, gasping for air. Then he threw up.

I waited until he was done. Then I dragged him backward by the ankles, as I didn't want any of his mess on me. His right arm stretched out along the sidewalk, and I walked over and stamped down on the back of the hand, snapping the bones. He wouldn't be squeezing anyone else's face for some time. I flipped him over and reached in to pull out his gun. I took his car keys and his wallet, too. I removed his gun permit and driver's license, and dropped the wallet back onto his curled-up form. I ignored his groaning. All the while, I'd kept an eye out to make sure his buddy didn't come up on me unawares, but we were alone.

I tucked the keys, license, and permit in my pocket. I not only wanted to make things difficult for him, I needed to give him a lesson he wouldn't forget. Hard guys like this are difficult to change, as they're used to the occasional rough play. You hurt them a little, it doesn't stop them. You need them out of action a long time, so they can think about their life choices. This guy had been close to shooting me in that alley, and I sure as hell didn't want another killer on my trail, or going after anyone I knew. So I had to put him out of the game.

I held the barrel of the gun and knelt down to twist his leg around. Then I smashed the butt of the gun onto one kneecap, and then the other. He cried out in pain, and I rapped him across the mouth with the gun butt, knocking out a few teeth in the process.

It was brutal, but this soldier had made his choices to get to here. Terrorizing women and possibly killing had been part of his life. If the law couldn't get to him, I could.

And the Holloways would get the message that I could play dirty and rough, too. They probably didn't meet many guys like me in their line of work, so it might just give them second thoughts. At least I hoped so.

I stood up, feeling the weight of his keys in my pocket, and wondered if his buddy was in the apartment. I smiled. Yeah, just maybe. I remembered how big and tough the other guy was, but hey, I had a gun now, if I needed it. I didn't want to use it, as I hated them, but also didn't want to get overpowered.

At the door of the apartment, I took a deep breath. Then I put the key in, unlocked the door, and pushed it open. Stepping in, I saw a baseball bat right by the door. These guys didn't take any chances. I picked up the bat and tiptoed inside.

The living room had a television going, and the big goon was watching it, sitting on the couch with his back to me.

"Forget something?" He didn't even turn around when he said it. Big mistake.

With the bat, I made more of a snapping bunt motion, rather than a full swing, as I cracked it against the back of his head. I didn't want to kill the guy, just mess him up. But his skull was harder than I gauged, and he didn't go down. So I had to give him another shot, a little harder this time. Now he toppled forward, crashing onto the low table in front of the couch.

I went around the couch and felt his pulse. Not dead, but out cold. I raised the bat and smashed down on his right hand, then did the same to the left. Then the kneecaps, like the other goon. Another enemy soldier out of the battle.

His gun had been out on the table, and I picked it up. I also felt for his wallet, pulled it out, and removed his gun permit and driver's license.

While I was here, I might as well look for evidence tying these thugs to the Holloways. I checked their answering machine, but there was only one message: "Need you to run by the house in K'port."

I looked around for a few minutes, and found a sawed-off shotgun and another two handguns. Bad boys indeed. I found a long duffel bag, and stuffed all the guns inside.

I combed the apartment, but couldn't find anything that mentioned the Holloways. Disappointing, but hardly surprising. Only amateurs left an obvious paper trail, and this group seemed to cover their tracks. Only they hadn't expected someone like me, so they'd have to adjust their plans. And that meant a nice opening that I could stick a monkey wrench into, and give a good twist.

I left and drove to a spot I knew that overlooked the ocean. No one was around, and I dropped the guns in one by one. Anything that brought death, like they did, I wanted out of action.

Now that I'd hurt their guard dogs, it was time to go after the Holloways.

CHAPTER 17

The main gallery of the Holloways was a converted warehouse along the Portland waterfront. There were plenty of people about, some on obvious business and some just playing tourist. It was a sunny day, so I got a newspaper and found a good spot to sit and watch the door, where anyone coming out would also see me. Eventually the Holloways would know I was there and have to do something about me.

I caught the gaze of a man who started walking toward me. Throughout a good part of my history, a serious-looking man in a suit has always meant trouble. I quickly scanned the surrounding area, but there were no other people who seemed interested in me. Maybe he was alone, or if not, his partners were keeping a low profile.

As he got closer, I could tell from the cut of his suit he was carrying a gun in a shoulder holster.

Definitely trouble.

We were out in the open, though, with people moving in and out of buildings, cars getting parked, more driving by, plenty of witnesses. And the guy didn't look like he was going to shoot me. At least not right away. He stopped when he was about twelve feet away.

"Zack Taylor. I'm Warren Fielding. Can we talk?"

"Depends. Who are you with?"

"Treasury. I'd rather not flash ID right here. Can we go someplace else and have a chat?"

I chuckled. "Your undercover disguise needs a little work. Out here among the tourists with that suit and a shoulder rig." A slight red tinge spread from up under his collar. He had an open face, intelligent eyes, and didn't look like a predator. Maybe he was Treasury, but I couldn't imagine what he'd be doing with me.

I smiled. "Okay, let's go to lunch. You buying?"

His lips pursed, then he nodded. "Sure."

We made our way to a little place that had open-air tables. The hostess handed us menus, which we set down without reading.

I spoke first. "I'll take a look at your creds now, if you don't mind."

He thought about it for a second, then reached into his pocket and took out a leather case. He slid it across the table to me. Inside was a shiny badge and an ID that had his name and proclaimed him an agent of the United States Treasury Department. It looked real enough, so I closed it up and pushed it back over. He tucked it away.

I was curious as hell, but wouldn't give him the satisfaction of asking first. I sat there with a slight smile, waiting.

He grinned slightly before turning serious again. "Why are you staking out the Holloways?"

I cocked my head. "Okay, that wasn't what I was expecting."

"What's your interest with them?"

"I'm trying to find somebody, and the trail led there."

He nodded. "Then we might have a problem."

A waitress came over to us. "Can I get you gentlemen something to drink?"

"Iced tea, please," I said.

Fielding smiled at her. "Same."

She smiled back, and left.

"A problem," I said. "Do tell."

"I spoke to a Lieutenant McClaren of the Portland Police," he said. "We wanted to find out more about you, what to expect when we talked."

I laughed. "I can imagine his response."

"He said you were an absolute bull in a china shop, that you caused havoc whenever you got involved with something, and that you were contrary and stubborn."

I nodded. "Fair assessment."

"He also said if we approached you, there was little chance you'd cooperate, but it would be better to do it sooner than later, because you'd probably just bust up whatever else was happening anyway."

My snarky response was cut off by the waitress returning with our drinks. She set them down, along with paper-covered straws. "You gentlemen ready to order?"

"I think we'll need a few minutes," I said. "It's so nice out here."

She smiled and left us.

I unwrapped my straw and thought it over while I sipped my drink. "You're investigating the Holloways, and you've got somebody watching them. They spotted me and raised the red flag. How'd you know who I was?"

He chuckled. "As many times as you've been in the papers? You've got quite a resume."

I waited for it, and wasn't disappointed.

"Goes back a ways, too," he said, a little too casually.

"So you're thorough," I said. "But that was a long time ago."

"Still makes for interesting reading. Carlo 'The Knife' Tortelli as your employer. Want to comment on it?"

"Why don't you tell me what you think happened?"

"I am curious as to how you went to work for a mob boss."

"Former. He'd been shot, which made him retire, and was a little skittish about guns. And with people who knew his former associates. Wasn't quite sure he could trust those around him, so he took on an outsider. I was doing a martial arts show in Vegas, and was good at close-up disarming, so he hired me to hang around and play bodyguard while he visited his girlfriend. Nobody talked family business around me, and I left when I got bored. Later, some other government guys in suits rousted me hard, thinking I could tell them something about Carlo's business. One guy leaned too much, and I reacted badly."

"Was the prison time worth it, for hitting him?"

"Not even close. But I was young and stupid. Especially for pleading out, on advice of my attorney. Haven't quite trusted any government guys, or anybody in suits, since."

"Point taken. So you disappear for years, and suddenly show up in Maine, once more involved with organized crime."

"They killed my friend. I came up to find out what happened to him, and ran across their trail."

He stared at me. "And?"

"And we all got a lot more than we bargained for."

He nodded. "So you stayed here, but couldn't stay out of trouble."

I shrugged. "Why don't we order?" I didn't like talking about my past.

We picked up our menus, scanned them, and ordered when the waitress came back. Fielding got fried clams, and I got the fish and chips.

I'd been around a lot, and liked to figure out where people were from. Fielding's accent was mostly gone, but there was just a ghost of hill country still lingering. He sounded like another guy I'd known long ago. "Kentucky," I finally said, placing it.

He looked up.

"Where you're from."

His grin looked a little rueful. "Harlan County, born and bred."

"Creates tough people. I'd guess Treasury work beats the shit out of digging coal."

"Any day of the week."

"So you're investigating the Holloways. Is it part of the art war going on?"

"Yeah," he said, but his eyes lied.

"Don't bullshit a bullshitter," I said. "Pretend you're back in Harlan, give it to me straight."

"Back in Harlan? No thanks," he said. "Okay, you're right, our office couldn't give a shit about who runs the art world here in Maine. The Holloways are running a bigger game."

I thought about it. "Overseas?"

"Full points. They're selling tons of American art to Europeans, Arabs, Asians. Some real, some fake."

"You working with Interpol?"

He eyed me. "You know a lot for a dumb troublemaker."

"I'm a good guesser. And I'm betting it's not just a bunch of fake pictures."

"You're right. That's just our leverage for investigation. They don't cheat the bad boys, just the suckers, people with money and no higher connections. Then they're using the money to bankroll bigger stuff. They're looking at arms dealing, drug running, wherever the big score is. And they're talking to some real players."

"This sounds too big for Maine."

"That's why they're here. Playing for pennies on the dollar. And no heat in small potatoes land. They can get away with it, and there's no competition, nobody they burn that has enough juice to make them stop. In Manhattan, there's a dozen or more just like them, better connected, and way more ruthless. Down there, they'd be bait. Up here, they're kings. And they're working on becoming emperors."

Our food came, and we dug in. My haddock was fresh, tender and flaky. Always get the good seafood in Maine.

I understood where Fielding was coming from, but I had issues, too. "They may have killed a guy."

"Almost certainly."

"Why not get them for that?"

"Knowing it's one thing, proving it is another. We have no jurisdiction on that. The FBI has other priorities, so we're stuck working what we have. We want some of the bigger scene players, the people they deal with. Millions of dollars in goods moving back and forth, and we want to know just where it goes. We figure we can squeeze them to get what we want."

"So in the endgame here, they might give you what you want and get a walk."

He shrugged. "If they get us enough, I suppose so."

I put my fork down, trying to control my anger. "A guy tried to kill me, and got put away for it. Then the Feds released him because he rolled on someone else. He burned down my business, and is out there somewhere waiting to kill me. And now you bunch want to do the same with these clowns. All they have to do is point you at other targets."

He looked uncomfortable. "They're the thread we pull to unravel bigger things."

"How long you been on them?"

"Two years, so far."

"So they get to destroy everything here, ruin lives, kill people, in hopes that someday they'll be your snitches?"

"In the grand scheme of things—"

"Yeah, I know, we little people don't matter. A few dead bodies are just the price of letting them do business. It's always the same. Nobody does anything until somebody important is disturbed, then you appointed guardians take action. A group of thugs our government paid and armed kills some nuns in Central America, that's just a tough break, right? A dictator that our government put in power tortures his people, and as long as we do business with him, he gets to keep doing it."

His face was tight. "You're off the track. That's not how we work."

"You're all part of the same machine, and it stinks. Look, I recently dealt with another guy who set himself up to be a king here, a Japanese businessman with ties to the Yakuza. He started pulling strings, making things happen here, and got away with it. Nobody tried to stop him."

"Actually, we *did* try. We were building a case."

I looked at him, taken aback. I thought it over. The light came on. "And the Holloways were doing business with him. That's what got you on to me so quickly."

He said nothing.

"So you have all this intel on them, but you never take action. You're always waiting for the big score, hoping that they'll lead you to the kingpin. You never have quite enough to make it stick. The guys above them have millions, grease some politicians, twist a few nuts, turn some handles, lawyer up, and out they walk once more, straight back to business."

He wiped his mouth with a napkin. "That happens."

"Or some business partner has them whacked, like what happened with Harada, and you've got a double handful of nothing for all that work."

"That's why we need the Holloways. One whole line of investigation got shut down when Harada was taken off the board. Look, you play chess. You know you sometimes have to sacrifice pieces for the win."

"People aren't chess pieces. Folks are getting hurt and dying. Doesn't that matter?"

"We do what we can. Look, we need you to back off the Holloways. We don't think they're on to us yet, but if you keep sniffing around, it's going to get their wind up, make them tighten everything."

"Already too late. I met them, and they realized I couldn't be bought or scared away. So they sent their goons to assault a woman I know, just to intimidate me, and they let her know that I was marked for killing if I hung around."

"So that's why you're hanging outside their gallery? To let them know they should come get you?"

"Yup. I heard that two of their goons got roughed up earlier today, and are now out of action. So I'm waiting for the next wave."

"That was you? Jesus, they must have really got to you. I heard they were messed up pretty bad."

"I'm not saying it was me. But it's an occupational hazard when you attack women and pull guns on people. Eventually, they'll run out of local people to call. Maine can't have that many pros. So maybe there's your opportunity."

"Look, these guys always deal with cutouts. They never give an order directly, but run it through layers of people. That's why they've been so hard to touch. Two of their street-level hired help contractors get taken out, it's no skin off their nose. They'll easily get two more, but someone else will bring them in. You are a very small fly in their ointment, but you could ruin all the work we've done. If they have you killed, they'll still go to ground for a long time, and we're screwed."

"So you want me to stop hanging out in front of their place?"

"For starters, yeah. If I have to, I'll get the Portland Police to arrest you. But I'd prefer it if you just went away for a time."

"Fine. Tell me where Steven Harris is, let me pull him out, and you can run your operation all you want."

"We don't know where he is. We don't even know if he's alive."

"Then we have a problem. I'm going to find him."

"Can't you be reasonable?"

"I thought McClaren told you, I'm not a reasonable man."

CHAPTER 18

When J.C. called and asked to meet, I was somewhat surprised. We hadn't parted on the best of terms after the clambake, despite the fact I'd gotten what I wanted because of his invite.

I met him at one of those watering holes he liked, a quiet, upscale bar with old wood and dignified ambiance. He had his habitual glass of expensive scotch, and the waiter brought me a club soda with a lime slice on the side.

J.C. looked me over. "You're still nursing a grudge, aren't you?"

I shrugged. "Yeah. A bit."

"Lottie Perkins is a very old and dear friend. Sometimes when you get people involved, they get put into danger. You don't mean for it to happen, but it occurs nonetheless. And I couldn't forgive myself if I caused Lottie to get hurt. I heard about the woman from the colony who was assaulted yesterday, after all."

"I understand your point," I said. "But I'm not happy about it."

"I'm sorry about that," he said. "And I was feeling a little guilty. So here's a peace offering." He brought out a file folder and set it on the table.

"What's this?"

"You said you'd met the Holloways. Here's some background information on them. Maybe something in there will be of value."

I opened the file and started leafing through the contents. Inside were articles, newspaper clipping, photos, and pages of data, company names, and more. It was an impressive collection that had taken some time, effort, and expense to put together. "This is great. Thank you."

He dipped his head. "So I take it I am forgiven?"

"I'll even buy your drink."

"Singular?"

"Plural. I need this. You'll never guess who paid me a visit earlier."

"Do tell."

"A Treasury agent."

"Ah, so they've finally caught up to you to discuss those cash windfalls you accumulated."

"Very funny."

"So what is it then? Counterfeit money?"

"He strongly urged me to back off the Holloways. Seems they've been targeted by an investigation for the last two years, and he's afraid I'll spook them and ruin the whole thing."

J.C. sipped his drink. "Well, when you read through the items in there, it's not surprising they're being investigated. I'd have figured FBI, though."

"Apparently, selling art is a great way to shift tons of cash, and the Holloways are shuffling it back and forth across the pond for bigger and better things. So the Treasury is trying to follow the money."

J.C. tapped the folder. "That explains a lot. When you dig down a little, it's obvious the Holloways are into more than just art. They set up dummy corporations all over the world. One of their companies sells assets to another one of their holdings, who then sells it to yet another. Tracking down what each company really owns and where it all went would take a team of accountants years."

"The Holloways even had something going with Harada."

"Ah, didn't see anything about that in my research. No wonder the Treasury wants you to go away, after how he ended up."

"Yeah, apparently, I mucked up that investigation as well. Even though he was killed for what he was doing to his associates, and I just happened to be around."

"But that's what you do. Stir the pot until something boils over." He sipped his drink. "Tell me about the woman from Lottie's colony who was attacked."

"Peggy was with me the night we tracked down Bosco. He took a powder, and I followed him. A couple of thugs fronted me in the alley, having been called by Bosco, and pulled a gun. Peggy came out, and they took off. Someone, probably Bosco, later ID'd her to the goons. They tracked her down and jumped her in the grocery store parking lot yesterday, which meant they were following her. Didn't hurt her, but she's pretty shook up. I hired Theo to hang out there at the colony and protect her."

I left out the part about tracking down the license plate, which was too close to why J.C. had been mad at me in the first place. I also didn't mention the part about assaulting the two thugs.

"Yes, Lottie told me you'd asked her about posting someone there. This time, I vouched for you."

"You should tell her something else. She hired a woman PI recommended by Abernathy to track Steven. The PI told Mrs. Perkins she couldn't find Steven. When I went to see her, I told her to call Mrs. Perkins and confirm that she should cooperate, but she clammed up. There's something very fishy there. I don't think she looked for Steven at all. Why would that be? It probably means Abernathy told her not to. I know Mrs. Perkins trusts him, but I think he's shilling for the Holloways."

J.C. looked into his glass. "She's known him a long time. She's going to be heartbroken. Do you have any proof?"

"Not absolute, but things sure are pointing that way."

"Wait a minute. What's the woman's name? The investigator?"

"Dolores King."

"That's it." He snapped his fingers. "Mason Carter did an article on her some time ago. If you can overcome your revulsion and talk with him, maybe you could uncover the connection."

"Think I'd rather stick my hand in a garbage disposal. Besides, he wouldn't talk to me anyway. Nah, I'll do it my way. I want to track down that PI, but I need to follow Abernathy, too, and see what else I can turn up. But I can't be everywhere, and protecting Peggy and the colony is more important."

"It certainly is. That place is Lottie's heart and soul. What with her having to kick that Bosco out, and Steven disappearing, well, she's been through a lot. And she was devastated when that artist drowned. So I took you to Sonny's to see if you could turn up anything. But I didn't want her meeting directly with you. You upset people. And put them at risk."

"She's been at war with the Holloways for some time, and nothing's happened to her."

"Too obvious. If they went at her directly, everyone would know it and be against them. They'd be finished. Their way, they can chip away at her a little at a time until there's nothing left. Or maybe they're hoping the stress kills her."

"I was going to hang outside their place and make a nuisance of myself. But our Treasury friend said he'd have me arrested. He doesn't want me anywhere near them."

"You don't like being told to back off."

I swirled the last dregs of ice around in my glass. "Plus I don't have a lot of faith in their process."

"Of course not."

"He said they've been working this for two years so far. How many more years will it be? These bureaucratic agencies can take forever. Then if funding gets cut, or priorities shift, or even some new director comes in, the whole case can go away in an instant."

J.C. shrugged. "At least they're trying."

"Yeah, well, in my bad old days, I saw a lot of mobsters go through their whole careers despite being under investigation by local, state, and federal authorities."

"You just have a distrust of the feds in general."

"That's another thing. Those guys just want leverage to move up the food chain. They want the Holloways to slip up so they can grab them and put the squeeze on somebody bigger, which gets them a promotion or a better posting. So even if the Holloways do eventually get caught, they could get a walk in the end."

J.C. nodded. "I can understand you having an issue with that."

"You think? Just because the last guy they gave a free pass to burned down my dojo and is waiting to kill me?"

"So what's your plan?"

"I'll play the game and stay away from a frontal attack. Big organizations have a lot of loose threads to pull on. I'll find some." I looked at the file. "Their goons had a message to stop by the house in Kennebunkport. Would the address show up in a search of places their companies owned?"

"Maybe. Go through the tax records in Kennebunkport and check against the list of company names. You might get lucky."

I doubted it, but it was all I had at the moment.

J.C. set down his glass and gave me a steady gaze. "I'd tell you to be careful, but I know who I'm speaking to. You have a way of driving people to violence. They already went after someone at the colony. Would they go after Allison to get you to back off?"

My mouth went suddenly dry, and I felt a cold chill go up my spine.

Dale T. Phillips

CHAPTER 19

Now that I knew Allison should have a watchdog as well, I called Theo to ask if he knew of anyone else in his line of work that was discreet and reliable. He volunteered for the duty, but I preferred to have him at the colony. I wanted someone lower-profile for Allison, and Theo was anything but low-profile. He gave me a number.

I called the guy, and met him later at a coffee shop down on Exchange Street.

"Bruno Davis," he said, putting out his hand to shake. He wore glasses, was middle-aged, and about five-foot-five, with everyday clothes. "Just to let you know, I watched you for about five minutes before you saw me."

"That's pretty good," I said, impressed. "Normally I'd have caught on."

"I'm non-descript, blend in with the crowd. Wanted you to know that if you need someone watched, they won't know I'm there."

"That's exactly what I need. I want someone protected, but don't want her alerted or spooked. So this would be covert surveillance."

"I'm your man."

"Suppose the bad guys show up. You ready for rough stuff? Got a permit to carry?"

"Got one, and know how to use a gun. You'd be surprised, though, how good I can be close up. Lotta bigger guys don't give me a second thought until they're on the ground, looking up at me."

I smiled. Good training like that usually comes from a professional organization. "So what branch of the military?"

"Army Intelligence."

"See some shit?"

"Enough. Got out while I could, when we stopped being the good guys."

I nodded. "Don't know how long this will last, and it could get boring."

"You don't have to say it. While on duty overseas, I watched a house in Germany for eight months. The other guys eventually started playing cards and reading magazines, but I kept up the surveillance, and saw the guy when he showed up. If I'd been dicking around, we'd never have caught him."

"Okay, you're hired." I gave him the background on Peggy's assault, so he'd know the kind of thing to look for. I told him about Dolores, in case they used a woman. I showed him a picture of Allison and gave him her address and where she worked at the hospital. He was familiar with Portland, and said he could tail someone in a vehicle as well. I got the impression he'd do a proper job. I handed him an envelope with some money inside.

He thumbed through it and nodded. "Theo says you're good. That carries a lot of weight in my book."

"Same here. Just keep her safe."

"As if she was my own mother," he smiled. I felt at ease.

With that detail out of the way, I drove down to the colony to see how Theo and Peggy were doing. I found them in the welcome house, laughing and playing Scrabble. Peggy looked far more relaxed than when I'd seen her earlier.

"Looks like you two are getting along," I said.

Peggy laughed. "Except this bastard is kicking my ass. And Scrabble's my game."

Theo chuckled. "Those triple-word scores can be a bitch, huh?"

"Just for that, I'm going to put you in the shitty cabin," she said.

"As long as it's next to yours."

She frowned. "You don't think they'd sneak in here at night?"

"Doubt it. But best not to take any chances."

"Peggy," I said. "Not to worry. Those guys, at least, won't be doing anything for a while but feeling their pain. I messed them up pretty good."

She smiled.

Theo looked at her, then me. "Busy day for you."

"You don't know the half of it." I filled them in on the Treasury guy, and how we were up against the Holloways. If something did happen to me, I wanted other people knowing what was going on.

"I've got something you can check out," said Peggy. "After those bastards grabbed me, I started thinking. Had to be Bosco who told them who I was. He's the only one who could have known. So I started calling around again."

"Peggy, you shouldn't."

"Why not? Nobody does that to me and gets away with it. Funny thing is, no one knows where he is. Hasn't been seen since that night, but guess what? Bosco St. Clair is not his real name, surprisingly enough. He was born Edward Munson. Had it legally changed after he went to art school here. And his parents live outside Augusta, not far away." She handed me a piece of paper with an address on it. "Maybe you can find the little prick there."

"Good work, thanks. Hey, if you're that good at turning up leads, you feel like checking some boring property records? I'll pay you."

"For what?"

113

"I've got a list of shell companies owned by the Holloways. I want to see if any of those names come up in connection with any houses in Kennebunkport."

Peggy looked at Theo. "You'd be with me, right?"

"Every step."

She smiled and turned back to me. "Sure thing, then. You won't have to pay me, though. If I can get back at these fuckers, it'll be my pleasure."

CHAPTER 20

The next morning I got a map and drove to Augusta, and was soon off the highway. It was not far to the Munson place, at least in miles. But it seemed years in the past, as I went by shacks that looked like they'd been thrown together by hillbillies a long time ago, and never repaired since. Once you got off the beaten track here, it was deep country. There was junk in the yards, rusted vehicles scattered like lawn ornaments, and the heavy hand of poverty everywhere. Augusta was the state capital, but only a few miles away, it resembled a third-world nation.

My directions took me down a dirt road, where I drove with the utmost care, so my car wouldn't bottom out. It ended in a clearing with a trailer. An old Ford pickup squatted next to the place, with a missing fender and front bumper. I parked and got out slowly, giving anyone inside a chance to look me over.

I knocked on the trailer door. It whipped open to show a man glaring at me. "What the hell do you want?"

"I'd like to talk about your son, Edward."

"I ain't got no goddamned son. Go away." The door slammed in my face.

I knocked again. There was no response. I knocked louder.

The door opened again, and I was looking down the twin barrels of a shotgun. The man's voice was cold. "You fuckin' hard of hearin'?"

"Easy now. Are you Mister Munson?"

"What if I am?"

"I'll pay you to tell me where Edward is. He may be in trouble."

He paused, but only for a second. "That ain't our concern. There ain't no goddamned Edward here. We don't know where that little faggot is, and don't care. He's gonna burn in hell. Now get off my property and don't come back."

"I'm going." I backed down the steps, my arms up in a placating gesture. He didn't lower the shotgun until I'd started my car.

I drove back down the dirt road, but found a side path and eased onto it, until my car was out of sight. I went to the trunk and took out my binoculars. I slathered myself with bug repellent, and started making my way through the woods back toward the trailer. I hadn't seen evidence of a dog, so maybe I could watch the trailer undetected.

I found a spot where I could see the place, and settled in. Two long hours of incredible boredom later, the man left the trailer, got into his pickup, and drove away. I made my way to the car and drove back down to the trailer. Once again I knocked on the door. I hoped I'd get a better reception.

This time a woman opened it. She looked old and tired, like all of life's vital juices had left long ago. "What kind of trouble is Eddie in?"

"He's mixed up with some bad people. He may be scared and on the run. I'm trying to find him to see if I can help."

"Why don't you come in, though the place is a mess."

Mess didn't begin to describe the chaos within. Stacks of newspapers and magazines were almost waist-high in some places. Open boxes of all sizes were strewn haphazardly about, and odd pieces of bric-a-brac stuck up like antennae. I saw piles of plastic containers and mismatched dishes, and smelled cooked onions and cat pee.

She looked about, and moved a tower of dirty clothes from one end of the couch. "Please, have a seat."

I saw the cat hairs everywhere, and certainly didn't want to sit, but did.

"I'm Eddie's mother. I wish we could tell you where he is, but we haven't seen him in over a year, and we don't have a number or address to reach him. You said you'd pay to find out where he is?"

"Yes, it's important I locate him. He has some information that may be valuable, and other people want it for themselves. Did he grow up here?"

"Yes, but he never really fit in. He was always drawing something, you know, always playing dress-up. He's an artist in Portland, now, but I guess you know that?"

"Yes, ma'am."

"Eddie went to the art school there, but the city changed him. He was ashamed of us, even changed his name, and wouldn't come home. He told us over the phone one time that he was a homosexual, living with another man. That's when Myron disowned him. I'm sorry he pointed the gun at you, but he's never gotten over that."

"Edward is your only child?"

"Yes, so it's been hard. I have the name he calls himself around here somewhere, let me get it for you."

"I already have that, ma'am. Do you know any of his friends in Portland, or other places?"

"Heavens, no. I'm afraid we no longer matter to him."

"I'm so sorry."

She pulled a tissue from the sleeve of her sweater and dabbed at her eyes.

I tried again. "Was there any place from the past he would go to if he was in trouble?"

"Not that we'd know of. He's not been seen in these parts since he left for art school. I think he likes to pretend we don't exist, that he's an orphan or something. I'm sorry, I wish I could be of more help."

There was nothing more to be learned here, and I wanted to get out. I stood up and took a twenty out of my wallet. "Well, sorry to bother you, then. I appreciate your time." I set the bill on top of a broken coffeemaker.

She stared at it like it was a life-saving medicine. "But I didn't tell you where he was."

"You would if you knew. I'll find him, don't you worry."

She looked up at me. "Tell him his mother still loves him, no matter what he's done."

CHAPTER 21

When I returned to Portland, there were messages on the answering machine. One was to call Lieutenant McClaren. Although I knew it wouldn't be good news, I figured I'd better get it over with.

His voice came over the line a few minutes later. "What did you get yourself into this time?"

"Apparently, a covert federal investigation that could go on forever."

"How'd you get mixed up with the Holloways?"

"I was asked to find someone by a relative. Didn't know I'd wind up crossing swords with the art gangland."

"You say you never plan on stepping in shit, but I've never seen anyone with more talent for doing so."

"Thanks. Let me guess the reason for our conversation. You were approached by a gentleman from Kentucky to do a professional courtesy."

"Indeed I was." The distaste in his voice was clear.

"And I'm guessing you don't appreciate it."

"I don't enjoy being told how to run my department. Especially when it's a plain exercise of muscle."

"All this angst on my account?"

"Hell, no. You belong in jail anyway, but it sets a bad precedent."

"Once again, thanks a lot."

"So should I send the uniforms for you now? Save time? And then you can get your red-headed lawyer down here to slap us with a harassment suit, and we can start the circus."

"If you know how it's going to play out, why bother?"

"Because this is Maine, so whenever anyone flashes a federal badge in our face, we're supposed to sit up and say yessir."

I actually felt sorry for him. He was a decent man, and didn't deserve getting squeezed on my account. "How about we make a deal? I'll stay away from the Holloways gallery for the time being, so you can say you scared me off, like you were supposed to."

"And I do what in return?"

"There was a death last year, down the coast a bit. Artist from the Ogunquit colony, supposedly drowned."

"And?"

"And he may have had some help in leaving this life."

He sighed. "And this is based on what, exactly?"

"I talked to the fisherman who found him. Guy was in regular street clothes, so how did he wind up in the water, when no one reported a person overboard, and no boats were missing? Plus, he wasn't one for the water. Yeah, I know, they'll say he was walking along the shore and a rogue wave dragged him under. And apparently beat him pretty badly on his face."

I could almost hear McClaren mentally cursing.

I kept going. "Sure, maybe the guy had fluid in his lungs, but you and I both know someone could have done that to him before they dumped him into the ocean."

"So who was he, and who would have done it?"

"I found this out by accident, as I was checking into other things. You know the Holloways are engaged in a war with Loretta Perkins? They're putting the squeeze on, and have their informers at the colony. This guy must have been caught in the crossfire, seen something he shouldn't have."

"So why didn't anyone raise the red flag?"

"Not everyone is diligent. Guy's found in the ocean, easy to say he drowned. But maybe they missed something."

"So you're putting this on the Holloways, right? Why isn't Mr. Treasury pursuing this angle?"

"It's not his area of interest. They're not FBI. His people only take notice when large sums of money shift around. That's how they build a case. You know they've been on those guys for two years? Probably be twenty more. The Holloways will die of old age before they see prison. But if they had this guy killed, I'd like to see them nailed for it. Screw Kentucky and his bean counters."

There was a pause on the line. "How come every time I talk to you, I wind up eating a shit sandwich?"

"Sorry, lieutenant, I'm just the guy who turns over rocks. I'm not responsible for everything that crawls out. You know how I feel about cops. And you know I'm only telling you all this because you're not the kind of cop to slough it off, because it's extra work and inconvenient, to say the least. You actually believe in justice, so you'll check it out. And if it was murder, you'll open a proper investigation, no matter who whines about it."

"This is something. I call you to tell you you're about to be arrested. Instead, you hand me a potential murder case, and I wind up working for you."

"Yeah, we make a beautiful team, don't we?"

There was a buzz as the line went dead.

Peggy had been the second one to leave me a message. I called her back. "Did you find something?"

"Nah. Theo and I couldn't match any name from that list to any houses."

"It was a longshot, but worth checking. Thanks."

"Did you find Bosco yet?"

"No, his parents haven't seen him in over a year. He seems to have cut all ties to them. They live in a backwoods trailer, and they're hoarders, so he may have wanted to leave that all behind. Plus, his father didn't take the news well when Bosco came out."

"Many don't," Peggy said.

"So it was a good try, but looks like a dead end. A lot of people would run home, but I think Bosco would like to pretend he didn't grow up there."

"You almost make me feel sorry for the little shit."

"He made his choices. Was there something else?"

"A couple of things you may want to look into."

"If they were trying to scare you off, I'd say they failed miserably," I chuckled. "I'm really glad Theo's there."

"I loved the Nancy Drew books when I was young," she said. "But now that I'm involved in a real case, I'd say it's not as much fun."

"So how else can we twist the screws on these assholes?"

"A few years back, there was a guy who started making noises about forgeries. Then he suddenly went away."

"Went away how? Died? Missing?"

"Just not heard from again."

"That sounds suspicious."

"Sure does. And did you know Steven was a talented copyist? He could whip out a perfect copy of a painting in a style that looked like the original. When I heard about this forgery thing from the past, I thought I'd call you."

"I'm glad you did. You got a name for this guy?"

"No, but Mrs. Perkins knows him."

"Sounds like I need another chat with her, then. What's the other thing?"

"Okay, so I've been trying to figure out where that little shit Bosco went. I mean everybody knows him, and I've called everyone I know in the scene, both in the art world and the other. No one's seen him; he just disappeared.

"But I realized there's one place he'd have to go. It's a store for art supplies. We have to work, and when we do, we always need good stuff. The place where we all go is this funky joint down on lower Congress Street." Peggy read off the address.

"So the owner there, Sue, is a stitch. Been there forever, a dinosaur, but also a real sweetheart with a heart of gold. Does the whole Gertrude Stein thing, mentoring upcoming artists. Sometimes floats credit for the ones who are going through tough times, which is most of them. Anyway, I asked her if she'd seen Bosco, and she said she had. He showed up last week with some scary-looking guy in a suit. She thought that was strange. And even stranger, he bought paint. Tubes of oil paint."

She seemed to be implying that this was significant, but I wasn't getting it. "What does that mean?"

"It means that he was buying for someone else. Bosco doesn't work with oils. But you know who does?"

I thought about it. "Steven."

"Bingo."

I found a place to park near the address and practically ran to the art supply house. It was crammed with everything an artist might need: easels, canvases, even anatomical models.

Behind the sales desk was an older woman with a spangled sweater, and cat's eye glasses on a chain around her neck, like a librarian. A cigarette completed the picture, dangling from the corner of her mouth.

"Sue?"

"Maybe," she replied. "Whaddya want?"

"Peggy called you about Bosco. She said you'd seen him."

"Oh, yeah. Been in here recently, bought some stuff."

"You said he was with someone?"

"Yeah, a galoot in a suit. Hey, that rhymes. Anyway, the big guy stays close, like he's a babysitter or something. Pays for all the shit while Bosco hangs back. I say, 'hey, Bosco, how's it going?'"

"What happened?"

"The big guy gives me a hard stare, like I did something wrong. I've known Bosco for years, but he just mumbles something. Thought it was weird, you know? The big guy didn't look like an art lover, or a regular lover. Maybe he works for a patron, but it was strange, gotta tell ya."

I nodded. "It's kind of important I locate Bosco. Could you give me a call if he comes back in?"

She shrugged. "If I remember."

"Will this help your memory?" I slid a twenty across the counter.

It worked for a lot of people, but she just laughed. "Keep your money, honey. It's age, not greed. I'll see what I can do."

CHAPTER 22

I found myself before the huge gates once again, rolling up to the palatial estate of Loretta Perkins. But this time, my greeter at the door was the big bodyguard. His face went white, a vein standing out on his neck. His left hand was clenched into a tight fist. "You and me got some unfinished business," he said.

"So you think it would have a different outcome?" I smiled. "Love to chat, but I need to speak with your employer. What say we table this discussion for another day?"

"Yeah. Another time."

He glared at me as I walked through the place. If he'd had Superman-like heat vision, I'd have been a cinder.

Loretta Perkins was in her library once more, still looking frail, as a shaft of sunlight gave her a halo.

"You are persistent, I'll give you that," she said, by way of greeting. "But I like how you stepped in to offer protection after Peggy was attacked. Here's a check to cover expenses."

"I'm not here for that."

"Then what?"

"A few years back, there was talk of some art forgery. What happened?"

Her mouth opened in surprise, then her face sagged. "Oh, the poor man."

"Who?"

"Why do you want to know about that?"

"Because we have missing people, and lives are on the line if I can't figure all this out."

"That may be, but it's a terrible story. You keep bringing up painful subjects."

"I'm sorry, but they keep popping up. Please, it's important."

"All right. A friend of mine, Norman Cyrus, called me a few years ago and wanted to have a talk. He'd uncovered several paintings, sold here in Maine, that he thought were forgeries, and was looking into it."

"Then what?"

"Then his wife was in a horrible car accident, and Norman retired from public life to attend to her."

"And nothing more was heard about the forgeries?"

"It was no longer important."

"And no one else looked into it?"

"It was all very hush-hush, you know. No one in the art world likes to talk about the subject."

"*I* would very much like to talk to him about it. Can you call him for me, so I can meet him?"

"He'd been through too much. It would be dredging up the past."

"Mrs. Perkins, I need to check this out. This piece of the past may somehow be tied to the present, and what's happening. It may save some lives."

She clucked her tongue. "I must say, you do have a flair for the dramatic."

A short time later, I was headed up the Maine Turnpike for the second time that day. I frowned when I passed Augusta, wishing Peggy had told me sooner, so I wouldn't have had so much backtracking. But that was the nature of what I did. So much wasted time running down one useless thing, only to find later I needed to return to it. This was information I should have had from the beginning. I hoped there wasn't a lot of other information Mrs. Perkins was withholding.

Past the turnpike, I drove up Interstate 95, noting that there were long stretches of un-industrialized forest. The trees seemed endless, and even the marked towns along the highway weren't very big. Once I reached the outskirts of Bangor, there were more buildings, but this was the second-biggest city in Maine, and it still wasn't anywhere near crowded.

Norman Cyrus had been an art professor at the University of Maine, up the road a few miles in Orono, but he lived in Bangor now. I found the address, off a side street not far from the airport. The house was a big old Victorian that looked like it could have used some paint and maintenance on the outside.

The man who answered the doorbell was stooped and looked to be in his seventies, dressed in a cardigan sweater, even though the weather outside didn't warrant it. His face was lined, the mouth turned down as if perpetually disappointed with life.

"Doctor Cyrus? Thank you for speaking with me."

He led me into a parlor and waved toward a settee. "Can I offer you something? Tea? Coffee?"

"No, thank you."

"Lottie said you needed to talk about the past, and it was very important. So what is it you drove all this way for?"

He was going to make me say it. "Art forgery."

He looked at me and sighed before sinking down into an easy chair. "Why are you asking?"

"Because it might matter a great deal to people that are being affected now."

"I see." His gaze shifted, as if he was searching the air for old memories. "Well, I suppose it's time, then." He took a deep breath. "It all started several years ago when Marianne Lehman showed me a painting she'd recently purchased in a private sale. I knew the artist's style rather well from my profession, and something seemed off to me about the picture. Nothing you could put your finger on, mind, but to the expert eye, there was something not quite right. I asked her about the seller, and she said the provenance was rock-solid. I shrugged it off, and assumed she knew what she was doing, so said no more.

"Then, a few months later, I was studying another picture from someone else, and caught that same feeling. This was another private sale, and I didn't say anything, as I didn't know the buyer very well. But he didn't have much of an eye, and I thought perhaps someone might have slipped him a forgery."

"Did you call the police?"

"Oh, that's not how we do things. Reputations are built over years, and there are layers of trust. One whiff of scandal and decades-old relationships can shatter. The wrong word can get you blackballed for life. Before making any kind of accusation, any hint of wrongdoing, you must know beyond a doubt. So I began my own little investigation."

"What did you find out?"

"The possibility that someone was slipping the occasional ringer in with legitimate pictures. But you must understand, no one wants to talk forgery. Not museums, not owners, not the auction houses. I could confide in no one. But I noticed a pattern."

"Pattern?"

"With the really expensive paintings, those costing hundreds of thousands, or even millions, there are authentication services. At those prices, the pictures undergo a rigorous vetting process. It's costly, but worth it. And even then there's an occasional surprise. But at the level I'm talking about, all the paintings were under six figures. Not something you'd send out, see what I mean? The ones I started suspecting weren't anywhere close to Old Masters or high profile, but a much lower tier of value. Semi-obscure artists, none too far back, that were no longer alive, but that had caught the eye in one way or another. Ones where you couldn't be certain beyond a doubt about exactly when the picture was painted, only an approximate range.

"And the buyers didn't have the most discerning eye. They were usually wealthy people who bought something nice on advice of a well-intentioned friend with some knowledge. Around the fifty-thousand dollar range. Collectors, but not professionals, do you see what I mean?"

"I get it. Folks with money who want something pretty for over the mantel, a showpiece that demonstrates their good taste."

"Yes, but someone else has to tell them if the value's there or not."

"Was it the same someone advising these people?"

"Oh, no, that would have been too easy. But in each case, I knew the purchaser wouldn't have had any idea if the painting was genuine or not. That's what I mean about the trust. And to tell the truth, it's opinion. These pictures were such that you couldn't say with a hundred per cent accuracy that they were completely what they claimed to be."

"So how did you know?"

"When you've done this for fifty years, as I have, you develop a sense for authenticity. Just looking at a canvas tells you its story."

"I know what you mean."

"And we also have the issue of studios. When an artist gets to a certain level, they gather acolytes around them. Students and those being mentored, who do what they can to copy the artist's work. Even one painted by a known artist might have had some of the base work, as it were, filled in by the students. It happens. There are some studios who wish to up the production level to make more money. So every now and then, you might see a slightly different hand in a picture. The picture itself is genuine, but you see how difficult it is to tell whether something is an outright forgery."

"But your suspicions grew."

"Yes, it's a fairly small community up here, as you might guess. You have a few reclusive collectors, but most are part of the larger community. What good it is to own a prestige piece, if no one sees it? So I noticed a brushstroke here and there that I thought might not have been the artist represented. One or two would have gone unnoticed, but I saw more of them, and realized someone seemed to be in the business of selling talented forgeries to carefully selected buyers. Those who would be embarrassed if it got out that they'd bought a fake."

"And the sellers?"

"Several different ones. People with good reputations, for the most part. So I couldn't tell who was behind it all, though I had my suspicions."

"Might that be a set of twins?"

He nodded. "You know of the Holloways, then. Yes, they had the ruthlessness and the lack of morals to do something like this, which, if it got out, would utterly destroy the market for mid-priced art in all of upper New England. So it would have to be someone like them that didn't truly care about art deep down."

"What did you do?"

"Lottie's been my friend and confidant for years. I called her and told her my suspicions, because I knew of her feud with the Holloways."

"What did she say?"

"She was shocked, at first, and didn't want to believe it. She said she wanted to consider it, and talk it over with someone, see if they thought if she should get involved. If one person makes an accusation, it can be written off, for a variety of reasons. But when more influential people rally to the cause, it carries a great deal of weight. If I brought this all to light, it would mean a very messy and protracted war, lives ruined. Lottie had to consider if it was all worth it."

"So what happened?"

"A week after I phoned her and told her, my wife Helen was in a car accident."

The hair on the back of my neck prickled.

"She survived, but became an invalid. The police said there was some paint on the side of the car, which means her car may have been sideswiped. But no one can say for certain."

"She can't remember?"

The professor looked at me for a moment, then stood up. "Come with me."

He led me to a bedroom on the first floor. He opened the door, and I saw a woman lying in the bed, hooked up to machines. It reminded me in a horrible way of Mrs. Harris, but this woman gave no sign of recognition that there was someone else in the room. I swallowed, and felt the thickness in my throat. I stepped out, and he closed the door. We went back and sat.

"So you see. She doesn't speak, doesn't respond. I had to take care of her, and nothing else mattered. I resigned from the university, and dropped what I was doing. It got terribly expensive, and we were in danger of losing the house, and everything else. And then an art foundation stepped in and said we would receive a grant to pay for her care."

"Funded by Mrs. Perkins?"

"No. By the Holloways."

I had a moment of disorientation. "But ..."

"I know. Why would they? They weren't friends of mine. I'm known in the art world, and there was an outpouring of sympathy, but this wasn't something they normally did. There was no publicity, just a service that handles all the medical bills. It's the only thing keeping her alive. At the time, I didn't question it, I was just grateful. But in the last few months, with not much else to do but think, I had horrendous suspicions."

I sat and said nothing.

"You understand, and you're shocked. I didn't want to believe it, either, but what else could I think? That they were buying my silence. That somehow they knew, and were connected to the accident, and if I was occupied and settled, I wouldn't bother to look into forged paintings any more, as long as we were taken care of. Yes, I came to believe that, and worse. Suppose it wasn't an accident at all? Suppose that what I'd done caused this to happen to the woman I loved?"

The professor started to break, and then caught himself. "This is my fault. As long as I say nothing, she stays alive."

The room was too quiet, with only the ticking of a clock to be heard.

My mouth was dry. "So why are you talking to me now?"

"The doctors say that she doesn't have much longer. It will be any day now. Without her, there's no point to my life any longer, so I imagine I won't last even a year after she's gone. And then it will have all been for nothing."

"So you're thinking that perhaps I can uncover the truth about what happened."

"Lottie said you were looking into the past, and I almost didn't dare hope. Because if the Holloways had anything to do with this, I want them to suffer, and am willing to destroy everything." He looked up. "Do you understand?"

The pangs of the past welled up within me, my own ghosts making themselves known. "More than you know. It was something similar that brought me to Maine in the first place."

He nodded. "Fate, then, after all this time. Perhaps this is the last act of a desperate old man. But who else would listen to me? Who would believe, and go to war against such powerful enemies? Lottie said you were something terrible, a force of nature that would not be stopped. That may be what's needed. They have reaped the whirlwind. So let it smash down the old order.

"Mister Taylor, I love art and the art world. It was my calling and my passion. But what is based on a lie, better that it get destroyed. You do what you have to, and when the time comes, I will come forward if you call, and give testimony."

He held up a hand. "There's more. I have a paper with four names and the paintings that I know are not genuine. There are others, but you'll be able to start with these. I don't know how you'll proceed, though. It's not as if you can call out of the blue and ask to check their older purchases for forgery. The sellers are listed for three of them, so you may be able to track them back to a source."

"That might do it. At least it's more than I have now."

"But I cannot give it to you while she's alive. You understand? While there's one breath left within her, I must keep her alive. But when I do give you the names, it is the destruction of years of love and work."

I appreciated what that meant. "Professor, I'll do what I can to find the truth. There are many scores to settle with the Holloways, but if I can prove this is one of their crimes, I'll see that they're called to account."

His eyes told me how badly he wanted to believe that.

Dale T. Phillips

CHAPTER 23

Driving back the two-plus hours to Portland, I wondered how the Holloways had gotten wind of what Doctor Cyrus had been doing, if he'd been as discreet as he'd claimed. He said that he'd called Mrs. Perkins, and the accident happened a week later. She would have conferred with someone, and I was betting it was with Abernathy. And if Abernathy was indeed working for the Holloways, even back then, the word got passed. As of now, he was my primary target.

I stopped off in Portland at a camera shop and bought a Nikon camera, a few rolls of film, and a telephoto lens. The guy gave me a lesson in how to use it all, we loaded it up with film, and I was ready to go.

I stopped at a nearby drugstore to buy a notebook and a pen, and I was ready for surveillance duty. I realized though, that if Abernathy spotted me, he'd recognize me and spoil my stalking game. So I grabbed a Red Sox cap, the perfect New England disguise. Then I passed a display of reading glasses, basically a frame with a slight magnifying lens. I kept trying different pairs until I found the right one. The mirror showed me enough alteration of my appearance in case Abernathy got a quick look.

Then back down to Ogunquit. It was dinnertime, and I donned my cap and glasses and blended in with the crowds, my camera attracting no attention in a seaside tourist town. I strolled down by Abernathy's gallery, and used the telephoto to confirm he was inside. Then I found a spot and waited, while watching the gallery.

The smell of frying food made my mouth water, and people walked by with all manner of comestibles: french fries, sandwiches, ice cream. It all looked good, and I had to quiet my growling stomach. I focused on the gorgeous sunset, and had a good excuse to be using the camera. I took my time and got some terrific shots.

After more than an hour of waiting, Abernathy emerged from the gallery. I noted the time in my notebook and followed. He walked two streets over, to a small lot. He stopped by one car and began removing a canvas cover. Underneath was a tiny red convertible, the standard car for older, insecure men having their mid-life crisis. I did a fast trot down the street to my car, figuring that I'd have time to get to it and be positioned by the time he got through the traffic. I didn't know for sure which way he would go, but there were only a few choices, and I picked the route back to the highway.

He came by a few minutes later. I let a car get in between us, and with traffic as busy as it was, he couldn't open up the sports car, so it was easy to keep pace. He turned south and drove to Kittery, going down toward the water. He pulled into the parking lot for Warren's, a big seafood restaurant, and I drove past, put my flashers on, and pulled to the curb, since there wasn't any place on the street to park, and a parking lot makes it too easy to spot a tail. I saw Abernathy hand the keys to a valet and go inside.

So he was in for dinner, and I figured he was in for a long meal with his dining partners. I didn't want to go in and chance bumping into him, so I went to find my own dinner elsewhere.

Two hours later, he came out, and I trailed him north. He got off the highway toward Scarborough, and we went through a series of turns until he pulled off into a driveway by a lovely, expensive-looking house in an area with a number of other pricey lots. I noted the address, and waited a bit. I drove past every few minutes, but there was really no place to pull over and reconnoiter on foot in this ritzy neighborhood. I didn't want to attract attention, so decided to come back in the morning.

Next morning, I saw Allison for only a few minutes after she finished her late-night shift. I'd checked in with her shadow, and he hadn't seen anyone taking undue interest, other than a few young guys checking her out. He'd decided not to tail her into the hospital, because of the abundance of security cameras. I agreed that she'd likely be safe there, with all the people around.

I tailed Abernathy for the rest of the day. He played golf, stopped by the gallery for a few hours, and had dinner. Nothing out of the ordinary, no skulking or secret meetings. The pain of surveillance is that you just have to hang around and hope for the best, but you get bored out of your mind. I thought of Bruno Davis, watching a house for eight months. That would turn me crazier than I already was.

But it didn't stop me from being at Abernathy's house the next morning. He drove to the gallery, and parked the car, putting the cover on. Because he didn't come out, I spent the day memorizing the little village of Ogunquit, until I knew every store on every nearby street.

At about five o'clock, Abernathy finally left the gallery and went back to his car. He began removing the cover, and I high-tailed it back to mine, and went to my position on the road. He passed a few minutes later. After a time, he took a side road, and I wondered where he was going. I hung back, as there were open stretches where you could see traffic coming and going for a fair distance. I saw him stop by the roadside on a particularly open piece. I was several hundred yards away, and screened by trees. I took out my binoculars, having replaced the ones that got damaged in another adventure, and my camera with the long lens. With a short jog up the road, I could see Abernathy in the distance, clear as day, and he had no idea I was there.

I waited about fifteen minutes, with almost no other traffic, until another car pulled to the opposite side of the road. I watched the driver of the second car get out, and got a flash of recognition. It was Mrs. Perkins's bodyguard. I wondered why they would choose to meet like this, when all they had to do was pick up the phone.

It very likely meant the bodyguard was also in with Abernathy, and was passing along info to the Holloways. No wonder Mrs. Perkins was having such a tough time in the art war, when those around her were feeding her enemies every bit of information. Since Abernathy had recommended the private investigator, he'd probably also recommended this guy to be her bodyguard.

I took some photos, making sure to get both faces in the same frame, and more of the cars and license plates. They spoke for about ten more minutes, then got back in their cars and drove off. I had to pass the bodyguard's car, but kept my head down, and didn't think he recognized me. I stayed on Abernathy as he drove back to his house. Then I watched until the lights went off.

CHAPTER 24

While watching Abernathy's house the next morning, I kept nodding off, and chided myself for being lousy at surveillance. I almost missed him leaving his house, but it helped that when he parked for long periods, he always covered the car, and spent a few minutes getting the cover on and off.

Abernathy drove to the Maine Mall, and swung around to a remote corner of the enormous parking lot, where there were no other cars. The Mall hadn't been open this morning for very long, so it hadn't filled up yet, as it did later in the day. Once more I pulled out my trusty binoculars and camera. With sightlines like this, it would be no trouble getting pictures, and I was far enough away that he wouldn't see me.

A black Lincoln Continental pulled up alongside Abernathy, and a man in a suit got out. They spoke for a few minutes, and I got some excellent pictures with the telescopic lens, including the license plate of the other car. I wished I could read lips. Then the man opened the trunk of the Lincoln and took out a gym bag. He handed it to Abernathy, said a few final words, and got back in his car. After he drove away, Abernathy opened his own trunk and put the bag inside. He spent a minute checking the contents, and I saw him tuck something inside his suit. He closed the trunk and got in the car.

Now I was really interested to see where he went. I followed Abernathy into downtown Portland, where he parked and got out. I got lucky and found a place to park around the corner, and came back to watch. Abernathy crossed the street and went into a bank.

I couldn't follow him into the bank, of course, so I thought for a minute. My heart was pounding with excitement. I got out and walked to the back of Abernathy's car. There were only a few people on the street, and no one paid any attention to me as I took out my Swiss Army knife and popped open the trunk on the sports car. There was the gym bag. I unzipped it and saw bundles of cash, lots of them, and it almost made me giddy. Zipping it back up, I slung the bag over my shoulder and casually walked away, leaving the trunk open.

Thief is an ugly word. It sounds like one of those Old English words. Maybe it's the life I lived, but I had few qualms about stealing from someone like Abernathy. I figured this money was for something bad, as most law-abiding citizens don't meet each other in mall parking lots and hand off sacks containing thousands of dollars. I'd pegged Abernathy as one of the bad guys, betraying a friend and getting people hurt. Maybe a lot worse. So, finders keepers. I considered it compensation for all the time and expense following him had put me through. And of course, there was the fact I was kind of used to liberating loose cash from bad guys, having done it on previous occasions. It was what kept me afloat since I'd come to Maine, and paid my extravagant medical and legal bills. I kept getting into trouble, and figured that since the bad guys caused my bills, they could at least be kind enough to finance them when the occasion arose.

Through the telephoto lens, I watched Abernathy come out of the bank. I saw his reaction when he saw the open trunk from across the street, and snapped a picture. He ran to his car, almost getting hit by a passing truck in the process, and stood looking down at his open trunk in what appeared to be mortal anguish. I snapped a few more shots, reveling in my revenge. He looked around as if seeking a person who might be carrying the bag, or someone who could tell him where the thief went. He ran up to a woman, grabbed her arm, spoke something, and pointed to his car. She shook her head, and tried to pull away. He spoke again, and this time, she yanked her arm loose. Even from where I was, I could translate her NO! Abernathy spun around, a wild look in his eyes. He was in utter panic, and I was enjoying it a bit too much.

He ran back and inspected the lock, then looked under the car, as if the bag had somehow magically transported itself. He stood up, hand on the trunk, and I saw him sag in defeat. He'd been in the bank only a few minutes, and must have figured himself to be the victim of not only a casual street rip-off, but the world's worst timing. Maybe he'd eventually get suspicious at the coincidence, but right now, all he could do was think about was how his money was gone.

He slammed the trunk down, but it wouldn't stay shut, as it had broken when I jammed my little blade into it. He slammed it again and again, his features contorted with rage. A few people passing by gave him the look they give to crazies on the street. He stopped, panting, and put his hands over his face. He looked to be crying, and even a bastard like me almost felt sorry for him. But then I thought of Mrs. Cyrus, and how Abernathy was the likely source of their woes, and my sympathy level plummeted.

He wiped his face with a handkerchief, and looked around once more. Beaten, he got in his car and drove off, trunk flapping up and down. I followed, with the bag on the passenger seat beside me. I had a crazy thought that I should pass him and toss out money onto his windshield, which would probably make him crash. Maybe he'd end up like Mrs. Cyrus. But I let the impulse pass, and merely followed him back to his house, where he'd most likely be making some very important phone calls.

CHAPTER 25

While I waited on the road outside Abernathy's house, I imagined he'd be making panic-stricken calls to whoever had given him the bag of money. It was going to be an awkward conversation for him. I wanted to be ready for the next piece of action, so I changed film in the camera, putting in a fresh roll.

Two hours later, he left the house, and we drove back to the Maine Mall, returning to the parking lot where the handoff had occurred. Creatures of habit, once they found a place that worked. The same black Lincoln cruised up a few minutes after we got there, and the same guy got out. But he didn't seem happy. He was of medium height, and wore a suit, and looked like a hood. I shot some more pictures as they talked. Abernathy waved his hands around, while the guy just stood there with his arms crossed. Abernathy's face got all worked up, and he jabbed a finger at the guy. The other man suddenly punched Abernathy in the gut. I got the shot of him doing it. The gallery owner went to his knees, as the guy stood over him and spoke. I got a couple of shots of that as well. The man turned and got back in his car. Abernathy took some time getting to his feet, his face a mask of sorrow.

He sat in his car for over fifteen minutes, probably running through his options, but it was unlikely he had any good choices. The bad guys don't care when it's you getting ripped off, as long as they've covered their end. Abernathy was on his own, and had to realize by now he was screwed, and not getting a replacement payoff or a refund.

Eventually he drove off, and I followed him to a car dealership. He was there for over an hour, and when he came out, his trunk no longer flapped as he drove. He went south, back to Ogunquit, and returned to his gallery.

Now I pondered what to do with a bag full of money, as I certainly didn't want to drive around with it, but I had no place to stash it. I'd used J.C.'s safe on a previous occasion, but I couldn't keep going there and asking him to hide stolen money for me. I couldn't leave the bag at Allison's. Banks had cameras and kept records of who came in and out to a safety-deposit box. I was a little too paranoid to bury the money in the woods or hide it someplace not locked.

In the end, I decided to get my own small safe. I had a storage space at one of those twenty-four-hour-access places, acquired a short time before, while I was following a drug dealer. Of course I'd broken into his space and liberated some money from him, too. I was going down a road that didn't make me feel good about myself, much as I made excuses that they were deserving of getting ripped off.

I found a place in Portland that dealt in safes for home use. I bought one and rented a dolly to move it around with. The money would have to sit in that space until I found something better. I got the safe positioned, locked the money away, and felt a little easier.

With that burden off my mind, I drove back to the gallery. After another hour, Abernathy left the gallery, and went north, back to his house in Scarborough, and I found a spot down the road a bit where I could observe who came and went. I really wished I had sight lines to the house, but if I could see the windows, they'd be able to see me, and the neighborhood just wasn't set up for a better position. I had to be content with watching the driveway, and catching Abernathy when he came out.

Two hours later, a maroon Cadillac came down the street, driving slowly. There was nothing unusual about a Caddie in this neighborhood, but there were two hard-looking guys in the car, and they seemed to be unfamiliar with the area. I got a few shots of their license plate, and watched them through the binoculars as they turned into Abernathy's driveway. Now I really wanted to see what was going on in that house.

They were there for over two hours before they finally left, and it was getting on toward dinnertime. I thought about following them, and decided it was a bad idea. Bad guys have a sense for other predators, and one of their own getting ripped off was a big red flag that someone was watching. They'd be on their guard. So I continued to sit and watch Abernathy's driveway.

Around five, a small red Toyota turned into the driveway, with a middle-aged woman at the wheel. Housekeeper, maybe, or a cook.

A few minutes later, a police car came screaming up the road, siren blaring. The cop car screeched into Abernathy's driveway.

Oh shit.

Another police car raced by, also stopping. I thought about leaving, but from where I was, there was no real way to tell I was interested in Abernathy's. Maybe I'd see something important. Another police car joined the fray, and another one came from the other direction.

I was watching one cop stand by the driveway to direct traffic, when an unmarked car drove slowly by, then stopped, blocking my view. It backed up until it was in front of me, and I was looking at Sergeant Lagasse of the Portland police.

He got out of the car and came around to my driver's side. "What are you doing here? As if I didn't know."

"What's happened?"

He smiled so wide, I thought his face might crack. "What's happened is, I finally gotcha. At the scene of yet another murder, and here you sit, watching the victim's house." He looked around. "Though it sure doesn't look like Christmas."

CHAPTER 26

The police station interrogation room in downtown Portland didn't look any better this time around. The first thing I did was lawyer up, and place a call to Gordon Parker, my expensive, flamboyant, yet crackerjack attorney. Then, for once, I shut up.

Parker came in and convinced them to give him some alone time with me. As usual, I marveled at his flaming orange hair, impeccable suit, and sheer magnetism. He looked me over like a disappointed father. "So what should I tell them about your being outside a murder victim's house with surveillance equipment?"

"Tell them to be damn careful with that camera. It probably has the killers on film. I got their plate number. And the guy who punched the victim."

He shook his head. "I swear, you test even my powers to keep you out of jail. Why were you on the scene?"

I gave him a quick version of what I'd been up to, and how I had to watch Abernathy because I'd been forbidden to do surveillance on the Holloways. I told of the man in the parking lot, and the two that had gone to the house. And I had to finish with a warning. "There might be a very pissed-off Treasury agent looking to hang me out to dry."

147

He sighed. "You managed to fuck with the feds again? Jesus, why do you do it?"

"Just lucky, I guess."

"This isn't funny. The boys from Washington play by a different set of rules. They tell the local prosecutor to go after you, it's going to get messy. And that police sergeant is practically tap-dancing for joy out there."

"What can you do?"

"Start with motive. What are they going claim is your relationship with Abernathy?"

I told him about the scuffle at the colony. He wrote it down, shaking his head as he did. "So they've got a motive, and they sure as hell have opportunity. Assuming you really didn't do it, can we safely demand an immediate test for gunshot residue on your person?"

"Yes, great. I'm clean."

"Praise God for small favors. Though they'll downplay that, saying you wore gloves and changed clothes. Anything incriminating in your car this time? Better if we give them permission to search, rather than go through the hassle of a warrant, which just makes you look guiltier."

I shook my head, even though I was now thinking about the bag of money that had been with me not long before. If it had still been there when they searched my car, even Parker couldn't have kept me out of jail.

Had Abernathy been killed over its loss? I swallowed, feeling guilty, but I still didn't want to go down for his murder. So I didn't tell Parker about it. The fewer people who knew about it, the better off I was.

"Good. We'll make sure to get another person to monitor as they develop the film, to ensure it doesn't get magically ruined. You better hope to hell you got good pictures. They might save your life."

"Doesn't it matter that I didn't do it?"

"Not really. If they focus on you out of the gate, they won't look too hard elsewhere. So we've got to put them on the mystery men you got pictures of. Cross your fingers and hope they're known to the cops. What's a good reason for me to tell them why you were there?"

"Because I'm looking for a guy, and he disappeared while working for Abernathy. And he lied about it."

"Excellent. That's something. You ready to face them?"

"I guess." My bravado was gone. "Please don't let them charge me. I can't go back in a cell."

He stared at me. "Then have you ever thought about changing your line of work?"

Parker told the cops we were ready to talk. Lieutenant McClaren came in, followed by Lagasse. I figured as long as McClaren was there, Lagasse would be in check, so maybe it wouldn't be too bad.

And then the bottom dropped out. Warren Fielding came in as well, looking like he wanted my head on a platter. He didn't hold back. "What part of 'stay the fuck away' didn't you understand, asshole?"

"Easy now," said Parker, raising a hand.

"Easy my ass," said Fielding. "Counselor, you may be a big deal up here, with your clown hair and all, but I am going to have your client's nuts in a federal wringer."

"Listen, you pettifogging pissant," Parker snapped back. It was the first time I'd seen him lose his cool. I guess he didn't like insults about his hair, or maybe just people from Washington. "I know you sycophantic cocksuckers from Washington think you're in every way superior to the hillbilly rubes, and can push us hicks around, but you by God are going to have my foot well up your ass if you think you're going to railroad this man. Does that get through to your arrogant excuse for a brain?"

The room was as silent as a cemetery. I think four of the mouths were hanging open.

Fielding had had the rug pulled from under him, but he gave it another game try. "Your client interfered with a federal investigation."

Parker fired back. "Ah, yes, your famous never-ending investigation. You people were dicking around for years, pulling your cranks and waiting for the big score. You had jack shit, and jumped my client for even looking cross-eyed at your subjects. Now someone else gets killed, and you claim he was the central part of your whole farce."

"We had a file ..."

"Well whoop-dee-do. While you were threatening Mr. Taylor with illegal harassment, did you also tell him not to have anything to do with Abernathy?"

"Well, not directly, but—"

"*But* my ass. Now you're claiming after the fact that he should have had *a priori* knowledge of every person under the scope of your investigation. And since you didn't share that information, it means only that you're mad, and want to throw someone under the bus. Well, you're just going to have to look elsewhere."

Fielding swallowed with seeming difficulty, his face all twisted with passionate rage. "Your client has an extensive prior record of violence."

"If you're referring to events of the recent past, yes, Mr. Taylor has been cleaning up some of the dangerous criminals allowed to roam free while you sit on your ass and file reports. Or maybe you're referring to the distant past, where some federal dickwad like yourself overstepped his authority, which *created* a crime. Want us to leave the two of you alone for five minutes, so history can repeat itself?"

I had never thought Lagasse and McClaren would have stood by and watched a train wreck. But Fielding knew he was beaten, and if he wanted to proceed against me without proper procedure, he was going to fight a rabid wolverine that would tear his guts out. Parker would harangue any judge if there was a hint of impropriety. Fielding had probably never met an adversary like Parker, and had made a mistake by insulting him from the get-go.

Parker pressed the advantage. "So let's test for gunshot residue, right now, and develop those pictures, while you're searching my client's vehicle. And unless you've got something better than a mere grudge against my client, I suggest you either charge him right now, in which case you'll see a suit that'll break you all, or my client is going to walk out of here while you look for the real killers."

I had to admit, Parker was worth all the money I paid him.

Dale T. Phillips

CHAPTER 27

Maybe I should listen to Parker, find another line of work.

Yeah, screw that.

I was who I was, a guy always finding trouble. Or it found me. I'd tried to go legit, but that hadn't worked very well. Maybe I had too much baggage. Or maybe I still had my self-destructive streak, and liked putting myself on the line.

In addition, I hadn't liked getting pushed around by the authorities once again, so that might have influenced my next bad choice. I headed south.

Ogunquit was no longer busy, winding down the day. I passed the gallery and saw the *Closed* sign on the door. The cops would be by to search the place, it was just a question of how soon. I hoped to take a peek inside and see if there was any clue to finding Steven.

I walked around to the back. There weren't any people around, but there were windows that faced the rear entrance of the gallery. I'd just have to take my chances.

When you skulk around, people know you're up to no good. But if you walk up to a door like you're supposed to be there, most don't give you a second look. My Swiss Army knife managed to open the lock in a short time, after slicing an alarm wire in the right place. I'd been there not much longer than anyone fumbling with a regular key, and there was no outcry.

Once inside, there were some lights on, so I kept out of sight of the windows on the street, making my way along the wall to Abernathy's office. I sat in the dead man's chair and started going through the papers on his desk, feeling like there was a sliver of ice on the back of my neck. I'd been to an estate sale once, and had had the same feeling while looking through things that people had left behind after they died.

There was a stack of catalogs and art magazines in the corner. I ignored those for now, hoping for more likely game. I found some correspondence in a basket on the edge of the desk, and went through each piece, hoping for any scrap of relevance. Nothing there. I opened the drawers one by one and examined the contents. That took a little bit of time. I pulled the drawers out, and checked their undersides, a good hiding place when you're in a hurry. No casual person is going to find something taped to the bottom part of a working drawer, but any half-decent burglar will automatically check there.

I heard voices outside, and froze. Was it the cops, or someone coming in to the gallery? Either way, I was totally screwed. Sweat broke out on my brow as I strained to hear. My heartbeat drummed in my ears as I awaited my fate. After what seemed like a hundred years, the voices broke off. I waited to be sure, but there were no other sounds. I started to breathe again.

I went around the room, to the shelves filled with books, knickknacks, and paraphernalia of all sorts. An hour went by, and then another, as I combed every piece of paper, every potential hiding place. The filing cabinet took a while to get through. Still nothing, and I was getting pretty discouraged. You'd think that a crooked dead guy could have a little more consideration and leave behind a nice fat clue.

154

Sighing, I went through the stacks of catalogs and magazines, quickly flipping through the pages and shaking each one. All I got for my trouble was a pile of paper insert ads.

I took a last look around, and saw the wastebasket. I pulled a chair over and started sifting through it. There were lots of crumpled and ripped pieces of paper, but nothing that had any sort of clue, from what I could tell.

And then I found it. A tiny scrap, of a different color from all the rest, stuck to the bottom, probably left over from when the basket had been emptied before. I gently pried it up, not thinking about what else might be attached by the stickiness.

Only the word *Kport* and a number. A telephone number. The last digit was missing, but I had most of it. And Kport was a house in Kennebunkport. I'd bet on it. I had a clue, finally. And I had someone who could help me track it down.

Dale T. Phillips

CHAPTER 28

The next morning, I picked up the phone when it rang.

"This is Sue, from the Art Warehouse. That package you ordered just came in, and is being kept safe. If you want it, you should come now."

I understood what she was saying. Bosco had just come in, and had his guard with him. I got in the car and raced downtown.

I found a spot to park and approached the place on foot. There was a black panel van parked just down the street, facing the Warehouse, with a guy behind the wheel, smoking. He did not look like an art student. Another thug of the Holloways? I'd bet his buddy was inside, hovering over Bosco while he bought art supplies.

I thought about how to play it. I could take the driver out, and wait for the other one to emerge with Bosco, but I didn't know if that would work. Maybe the guys wouldn't talk, and maybe Bosco didn't know the address of where Steven was being held. Or maybe Bosco would run like a rabbit while I was fighting the guard, like he had before. These guys were my only real lead.

I wanted pictures of the van and the license plate, but the cops had seized my camera, and I hadn't gotten a replacement. I went back to my car and jotted the number down on a scrap of paper, then waited. After maybe fifteen minutes or so, another big goon came out from the store, with Bosco in tow behind him. The guy in the van started the engine. The thug opened the back door of the van, and Bosco put the bags inside, and climbed in. The thug went in after him. After a minute, I saw the thug move from the back to the passenger seat beside the driver, and they took off.

We left Portland and headed south, and I was not surprised to see us wind up in Kennebunkport. Where the road swerved to parallel the ocean, there loomed the white structure of the old Colony Hotel, no relation to Mrs. Perkins' colony. My friend Ben had worked there one summer long ago, before he'd come back to Maine and gone to another resort, Pine Haven, further up the coast. I made a note to go visit his grave at the Portland cemetery when this business was done.

Out on the rocks as I drove along the winding shore road were artists with easels set up to paint the seascapes they sold to tourists.

A few more twists and turns, and the van pulled in at a driveway next to a lovely house by the sea. It squatted on the shore, not the biggest place by any means, but not a cottage, either. It would be worth a couple million just because of the location. Ben had told me some of these houses were built by Old Money, some by New Money, and some by Drug Money, as the coastline and plethora of boats made smuggling popular.

Using my binoculars, I saw the passenger-side thug get out and go around to the back of the van. He opened it, reached inside, and brought Bosco forth. With a bag over his head. Guess they didn't want him to know the location. I sure wished I'd had my camera for that shot.

The thug didn't remove the bag, but guided Bosco to the front door, and rang the bell. The door opened, and another guy had a look around before he let them in. The thug came back out, got the bags of art supplies, and returned to the house. The van started, and pulled away.

Much as I wanted to know where the van returned to, I had the house in my sights now, and thought there was more interesting game here.

I scanned the area, but didn't see a real place for long-term surveillance. You couldn't park for long, or the cops would come by and ask what you were doing. Rich towns get better protection from outsiders. Not to mention that the political Bush family had an estate not far down the road. So I didn't want to attract attention.

I drove past, but didn't see any place from where I could watch the house. These summer getaways of the rich were fat targets, and the cops would spot someone who looked like they were casing a residence. I turned around and drove back, wondering where I could find a spot to stake out the place.

As I passed the artists again, I had a flash, pulling the car over to the side. I could see the house from this point. With an easel and a paintbrush for cover, I could be out on these rocks all day. I could even use my binoculars without anyone thinking it out of place.

Four artists were scattered about, two men and two women. I jogged over to the closest woman. "Hello there," I said. "I'm sorry to bother you, but this is the perfect spot, just what I need to compose my piece. I like what you're doing there. I can't do anything close to that good, but I wonder if it's possible to get permission to set up here like you've done."

The white-haired woman stopped dabbing at her canvas and looked me up and down. Maybe I didn't much look like a painter, but so what? If I said I was, then I was.

"Randall Kincaid. How do you do?" I said, and extended my hand. But she didn't shake, holding a palette in one hand and a brush in the other. "Like I said, sorry to bother you, but I've just got to try this spot. The light is amazing."

"It is," she said at last. "Anyone who comes here, though, has to mind their manners."

"Oh, I'd keep to myself," I said. "Where does one park?"

She pointed her brush at four parked cars in a patch of grass on the other side of the road. "You've got to get here early, if you want to be sure of a place. Park anywhere else along here, they'll tow you. Otherwise, you have to walk in from town."

"That's why I asked. Thank you. I think I'll come out tomorrow morning."

And I had my surveillance spot, but I couldn't stay there yet. Since the van had driven off, I thought Bosco and his guard dog might be staying the night. I drove back to Portland, pleased with my cleverness.

Allison was at home. "I need to become an artist," I said. "What?"

"I need to look like one of those seaside painters, down on the rocks at Kennebunkport. I can look like I'm painting all day while I watch a house."

Her brow creased as she looked at me. "You want me to teach you to be a painter?"

"No, just make me look like one. You've still got all your old supplies, right?"

"They're up in the attic." She glanced upstairs and sighed.

"Can we get them? Please? I need to see what's going on in that house. Who comes and goes. It could be important."

"Another one of your shenanigans."

"That's a good word." I fell silent, and she looked at me. I could tell I'd need to make this up to her, for being such a pain in the ass. I followed her up the stairs and then up the ceiling steps to the attic. She turned on a light. There were drop cloths spread over a number of items, and she looked around, hands on hips.

"I think it's all over there." She went to a corner and started lifting drop cloths and looking at what was underneath. "This is it."

She started handing me things. "That's probably all you'll need."

We got downstairs, and I looked at our haul. A canvas and easel, a box of paints, with brushes and tools, and a palette. Her face had a strange expression, and she reached out to touch the canvas. I could tell the sight of all the things with which she had pursued her passion was stirring up feelings and memories.

"How long has it been since you've painted?" I watched her.

"I put all this away when Mom got sick. Just never got started again."

"Never too late, you know."

She made a noncommittal sound.

"I should take something to sit on, too. And I better dig the cooler out."

"There's other artists out there, right?"

I looked up. "Yes, but only a few."

"True, but if anyone comes over to look at your work, they'll know you're not there to paint. Wouldn't that make them suspicious?"

My face fell. "I don't suppose I can just dab away to get something on there?"

She laughed. "If you want to look like an idiot."

"What should I do?"

She handed me a tablet of paper. "Use this sketch pad. Set up all the other stuff, but just stick to the sketchbook. If someone asks to see, close it up and tell them you don't show preliminary studies. A lot of artists are touchy about that, so you'll be fine."

"Sounds good," I nodded. "Thanks."

"Well, if you're all set with your spy gear, I'm going to go take a shower."

"Need any help?"

There was only the faintest upturned corner of her mouth. "Maybe."

Dale T. Phillips

CHAPTER 29

The next sunrise showed a clear day, all blue sky and promise. I packed a lunch and all the gear, including my trusty binoculars, and drove down to the rocks by the sea. There were still two parking spaces left in the tiny area, and I inserted my car into one of them. I took out my equipment and walked across the road, giving a small wave to the two artists already there. It took me some work to set up the easel on the irregular rocks, trying to keep the tripod legs even and stable. The wind blew it over twice, until I wedged it tight with stones. It made me feel like an idiot, and made me feel like I was getting unwanted notice. I took out a small canvas, but realized it would never stay on the easel, unless I had clamps of some type. I rummaged through the gear and found a couple, and finally secured the canvas. Taking out my sketch pad, I sat in the canvas-backed director's chair.

Every so often I casually scanned the sea with my binoculars, and if my gaze strayed to my left to take in a certain house, I hoped it didn't seem too noticeable. A third artist walked by me, giving me a once-over. I nodded, and she went past. She set up her easel about seventy yards away, looking my way every couple of minutes. I tried to ignore her and look like I was sketching, but I felt like I was being watched, not being the watcher.

Half an hour later, I looked up and saw a huge round man picking his way over the rocks with that peculiar grace displayed in some large people. He was dressed in black and carrying a long, slim wooden box. He wore a fedora like those sported by Alpine hikers, right down to the feather in the hatband. He probably thought it looked jaunty, but on his huge head it looked small and ridiculous.

He stopped next to me. His face was mottled red, contracted in anger, his thick lips mashed together in a tight line. He was huffing like a faulty engine. I closed my sketchbook before he could see my doodles.

"Who the fuck are you?" He had an arrogance in his voice like he was used to pushing people around.

"I beg your pardon?" I didn't need this kind of attention.

"I said, who the fuck are you? You're in my spot."

I looked around. "There's plenty of space here."

"Don't get funny with me. My parking spot. You took it."

"Ah," I said. "I was told it was first come, first parked. Sorry."

"Move your car."

"What?"

"I said, move your car." He took a step closer, as if to intimidate me with his bulk. "Don't make me tell you again."

"You're late," I said. "By at least half an hour. If you'd gotten your lazy ass here earlier, you'd have had your spot. As it is, now you're going to have to walk a bit. Probably a good thing, in your case."

The skin around his eyes scrunched up, making them look narrow and mean. "You can't talk to me like that."

"I think I just did. So unless you're going to sit on me, buzz off and leave me alone."

His face went through some contortions, as the realization dawned that he wasn't going to get his way. "You don't belong here."

164

"And yet, here I am. Physical point of fact."

"But that's my spot," he wailed like a spoiled child.

"That's the funny thing about public spaces. They don't belong to any one person."

"You can't just take my spot."

"I took a spot. I didn't take your spot. Your name wasn't on it." I felt ridiculous, arguing with this entitled man-child.

"But I'm here every day. I've never seen you here before."

"That's not my problem. But you are. Go away now, and get here earlier tomorrow."

His features rippled again, and his lower lip quivered, as if he was going to cry. "You'll be sorry."

"I already am. Bye now."

His bulk shook in a giant tremor, his jowls wobbling in outrage. He turned and made his way back over the rocks, daintily stepping his way over the uneven surface.

I took another look through the binoculars. There was no movement over at the house. I opened my sketchbook and looked at the childlike drawing I'd scrawled. Artistic talent of any sort always amazed me, whether painting, drawing, or even the ability to create music.

The older woman was coming near. I sighed and closed up the sketchbook again.

"I take it Elliott did not get you to move your car," she said.

"Funny thing is, if he'd asked nicely, I might have considered it."

"Elliott never asks nicely. He's an asshole."

"I gathered that."

"Haven't seen you here before."

"I came out yesterday," I said. "It's so beautiful, I had to come get some inspiration."

"Where are you from?"

"California," I said. It was the truth. I'd been born in Fresno.

"May I see?" She indicated the sketchbook.

"They're just preliminary sketches. I never show unfinished work." I smiled.

"I see. What's your primary medium?"

I knew enough from talking with Allison to get what she was referring to. "Oils."

"Ah. Mine is watercolors. Will you be coming back tomorrow?"

"Yes."

"Well, Elliott might have something to say about that."

After a grilling that would have done credit to Lieutenant McClaren, the nosy woman eventually left off interrogating me to go back to her watercolors. Nevertheless, she kept looking over at me until I turned the binoculars on her, which made her suddenly go back to her business.

Then I watched the house. Nothing moved.

About an hour or so later, Elliott came back, picking his way over the rocks. With him walked a big Nordic-looking blond guy with a wife-beater T-shirt that showed a lot of muscles. Tattoos went down both arms, and he had a gold earring. I guessed what he was here for.

"Seriously, Elliott?" I said as they drew near. "You want a fight over a parking space?"

"This is Tomas," wheezed the round man. "He'll escort you back to your car."

"Let me guess," I said to the muscle. "You're a painter, too."

"Let's go," the voice that came from the big Viking was pure gravel.

"No, I kind of like it here, despite the distractions. Tomas, if you assault me, I will defend myself."

The blond smiled as he stepped in and reached for me. He had at least five inches of height on me, and a lot more weight-room muscle, but he was expecting a compliant artist, someone who was no match for his strength and size.

I grabbed his outstretched wrist and stepped back, using his momentum to pull him with me as I twisted the arm. He was completely off balance, and I spun him in a half-circle and pushed him toward the edge of rock. It was a fall of only about six feet, but he shrieked as he went over as if it was a cliff. There was a cry of pain when he hit, and I went over to check the damage. He was wedged between two big rocks, moaning piteously and holding an injured arm.

Elliott had come to the edge as well. His face was ashen as he turned to me. "You monster!"

"You better go help him out," I said.

Elliott had a tough time getting down to where his friend was. He was agile enough on a flat surface, but climbing was not his thing. He took some time to get down the few feet and clumsily tugged on Tomas, whining and clucking sympathy all the while.

I glanced up and saw the other three artists arrayed along the edge, further down. I guess this was more excitement than they were used to. I stared at them, and they all looked away. I doubted I'd get more questions after this.

I went back to my sketch pad and binoculars. It was a good fifteen minutes or more before Elliott and Tomas were able to get up onto the rocks at my level. Tomas held one arm with his other, and his face had got a bit banged up. He was limping, too.

"Hey Elliott," I called out. He turned his gaze toward me. "I'll only be here for a day or two, and when I'm gone, you can have your spot back. But until then, I don't want any more problems with you, so why don't you take a break. You can nurse Tomas back to health."

Elliott glared at me and cursed under his breath. But they left.

After another hour, the black van drove up and parked in the driveway. The driver went to the door and rang, then went back to the van. A few minutes later, the thug came out with Bosco, hooded like before. He opened the back and got Bosco in. The van drove off, and I let it go. I didn't want to push my luck by following with the same car as I had yesterday. They might get suspicious.

There were still two cars in the driveway, and possibly another in the garage, so that could mean at least three hostile guys in the house. Too many for me to storm the place.

A few hours went by, and nothing else happened. I ate my lunch and watched the house. I had to go over behind the cars to pee. I don't know what the others did, but they left from time to time. Maybe they had a secret club bathroom.

In the early evening, right around dinnertime, a car pulled away from the house. There was a man and a woman, she wearing a big scarf over her hair, and huge sunglasses. They came back half an hour later. When they went into the house, the woman was carrying several brown paper bags. Dinner?

I was thinking about dinner myself, my stomach rumbling for attention and feeding. The artists had long since packed up and gone when the light faded, ignoring me as they left. After what I'd done to Elliott's friend, maybe they were afraid of me.

I'd hoped to see into the house, but they had drapes or shades to cut out all interior visibility. The mosquitoes were out in force, and I was trying to slap them one-handed while using the binoculars with the other. I eventually gave it up as a lost cause.

But I'd be back in the morning. Waiting for my chance to go busting in, playing the hero.

CHAPTER 30

The next morning, I was out at the parking area by the time the sun came up. I didn't want any problems in case someone decided to make sure I couldn't park there. No one else had shown up yet. I sat in my car, eating a fast-food breakfast sandwich and drinking coffee, though just a small one. I didn't want to have to take a leak every few minutes.

When the sun had warmed things up a bit, I got out and took my gear out to the rocks. I used the binoculars to scan the house. No signs of life.

I was tired of waiting and watching, and wanted some action. Though even I wasn't stupid enough to take on all the guards inside the house, I figured I could handle two. If two of them left, I could ring the bell and surprise the one who opened the door, put him out of action, and deal with the one that was left. Those were odds I could handle.

But what if the woman answered the door? I was still Old School enough to not punch out a woman, so that left me a potential dilemma. I'd need a plausible reason to show up at the door, in case I had to beat a hasty retreat without busting someone up.

While I watched the house in the morning coolness, I mulled it over. The day wore on, and three of the usual artist

169

crowd showed up, though none were talking to me. I didn't mind them leaving me alone: in fact, I preferred it that way. It let me watch the house and think. I ran scenarios in my head on how to appear at the door. Without any costume or disguise, I'd need something pretty basic.

Flowers. I could deliver flowers. It would at least get the door opened, while someone tried to figure out who they were for, and who sent them. Not great, but plausible enough. I wouldn't need any kind of delivery uniform, and better yet, a bouquet might hide my face. I liked it.

I didn't know if anyone was leaving the house today, but I'd have to take a chance. I jogged a short way towards town and found a payphone, and glory be, there was still a phone book attached. Only in Maine.

Checking through the Yellow Pages, I saw the listings for several florists. I called one and ordered a bouquet, and carefully explained where I wanted it delivered. I had to tell them twice. They accepted my credit card information, and said they'd be out in about half an hour. I hung up and jogged back.

In fact, they were there in about twenty minutes. The truck had pulled in behind the artists' cars, and I crossed the road and met the deliveryman. I took the bouquet and put it in my car. Then I went back to the rocks, ignoring the looks from the curious artists. I picked up the binoculars once more and studied the house.

About two hours later, I saw two men walk from the house to a car and get in. I hoofed it back to my vehicle, and waited for them to pass. Then I pulled out and drove over to the house. I parked in the driveway so no other cars could get out or in, and removed the flowers.

I went up to the door, ready for action, and rang the bell. I heard noises from within, and leaned on the bell some more. After a short while, the door opened a crack. "Yes?" It was a woman's voice.

"Flowers, ma'am." I kept the bouquet between us, hiding my face.

"We didn't order any flowers."

"Well, someone did. I'm just the delivery guy."

"You must have the wrong address."

I recited the house number in a bored tone. "Look, we got a call. Here they are."

"Wait, I know you," she said, and I realized it was Dolores King, the lady PI. I didn't give her a chance to close the door on me. I butted in with my shoulder, and pushed her back hard, sending her sprawling. There was the other guard, shouting and reaching for a gun in a shoulder holster. I threw the flowers at him and charged. I hit him and drove him back, into a sofa. We wrestled around a bit and I got him with a short hook to the jaw. His eyes went glassy, and I rolled away and to my feet.

What I didn't expect to see was Dolores standing there holding a gun on me. Stupid, chivalrous me, not hitting her when I had the chance. She was standing back far enough that I couldn't rush her. She had a wild look in her eye, and I feared she might pull the trigger by accident. It was a small gun, true, but it could still do the job.

"Get your hands up," she barked. I complied. But I'd better think of something fast, or I was a dead man.

"What are you doing here?" Her voice was brittle.

"I'm here to rescue Steven. Where is he?"

"I'm here," Steven called out, appearing on the staircase. He started down.

Dolores swerved the gun barrel for just a moment, and I tensed, ready to spring. Low odds, but better than nothing. But she swung the gun back to cover me.

"Go back upstairs," she called out to Steven.

"Stay here, Steven," I said. "So you can watch her murder me in cold blood. Then she'll have to kill you, too."

"Shut up," she said. Then she looked at Steven. "I told you to go back upstairs." She was moving the pistol back and forth, seeming to have trouble tracking the two of us. I needed the distraction that Steven provided. He was closer to her, frozen on the landing. I needed him moving.

I spoke loud enough so they both could hear. "You going to shoot him if he doesn't? Kill the goose that paints the golden eggs?"

"Shut your goddamn mouth."

"Was murder something you signed up for? I can understand you doing a little babysitting, but murder's a whole new game. You ever kill anyone, Dolores? It leaves a mark, you know."

She wiped the back of one hand across her mouth. I could detect a slight tremor in her outstretched hand. Even light guns get heavy if you just hold them out there. But crooking your arm for a more comfortable position means your aim is off.

I went on. "Steven, no matter what she tells you, after she shoots me, she can't let you live. She has to have you killed, so you can't testify against her. They were probably going to do it at some point anyway, but now they'll make sure of it."

"That's not true," Dolores said. "We have Bosco, after all, and Steven doesn't want anything to happen to him, now, do you, Steven? Especially after your conjugal visit."

"You bitch," Steven said, low and guttural. "You better not threaten him."

I saw my chance. "Then you haven't heard?"

Both of them looked at me. "Bosco's dead. They gave him a little reward for services rendered, and he OD'ed. There's no more reason to keep you alive, Steven. That's why I had to come now."

Dolores looked confused, then fear took over. Steven shrieked and lunged off the bottom step at her, and I moved. She clubbed him with the gun, and he went down. But I was close enough now, and grabbed her gun hand as she fired. The bullet went into my leg, and the crack of the gunshot hurt my ears. My other hand shot up with a palm strike to her chin, and she fell, out cold. I pulled the gun from her slack hand, and limped to Steven. He had a bad gash on the side of his head, and blood was everywhere. He was sobbing.

172

"Relax," I said. "We're alive. Let's get patched up." I found some paper towels in the kitchen, and made a wad compress and pressed it to my leg. I set the roll next to Steven and called emergency, and told them to bring an ambulance and lots of police, and to call Lieutenant McClaren. Then I called Gordon Parker. I had called him so often, I remembered the string of digits. I told him to meet me at Maine Medical.

I was feeling light-headed already, and the leg was starting to throb, so I sat next to Steven. He was still bawling.

I handed him a clean wad of towels. "Steven, Bosco's fine."

He looked at me. "He's alive?"

"Yes, I had to say that, or we'd have been killed. You saved us by distracting her."

"She could have shot me!"

"She was following orders to keep you under wraps, not shoot you. But she would have had to, if she'd killed me. It was our only chance."

"I'm bleeding." He looked horrified as he checked his bloody hand.

"It's not that bad. Head wounds bleed a lot. Press the towels against it. You're free now."

"You called the police, didn't you?"

"Yeah. If you're worried about illegal activity on your part, you can testify against these people, and probably get immunity."

"But they'll kill Bosco."

"They won't be doing any more killing. Bosco will be fine. They'll put him in protective custody until these people are behind bars."

"You're sure?"

"Cross my heart. Now let's get that bleeding stopped."

Dale T. Phillips

CHAPTER 31

Dolores had shot me with a small-caliber pistol, and the bullet hadn't smashed a bone or hit anything vital. I was lucky. Two inches one way and it would have split my femoral artery, and I'd have quickly bled to death. As it was, I'd managed to wrap the wound so I hadn't lost too much blood, though I was still a bit woozy, partly from the blood I'd lost, and partly from the lovely painkiller they'd given me.

A uniformed cop had ridden in the ambulance with me, as they still hadn't got it all sorted out. I was taken to Maine Medical in Portland, and Lieutenant McClaren of the Portland police slammed his way in while they were patching me up.

"Another goddamn shooting, and you're there? Do you try to get shot every week?"

Gordon, my attorney, swept into the room a moment later, with his shock of bright orange hair. The cavalry had arrived, for which I was grateful, as my recent relations with the law were likely to degrade the conversation rapidly.

Gordon and Lieutenant McClaren nodded to each other.

"Counselor," said McClaren. His mouth looked like he'd bitten a lemon.

"Lieutenant," Gordon replied, nodding. "Before you start grilling my client, may I have a word with him? I'd just like to see that he doesn't say anything untoward, since he may have impaired capacity from his wound and the drugs he's received."

"Oh, he's impaired all right." McClaren shot me a last glower and stepped outside.

I looked at my high-priced attorney and gave him the quick rundown, one that should only cost me a couple hundred. He asked a few questions and seemed satisfied that I wouldn't stick my foot in my mouth enough for them to arrest me for anything. He called McClaren back in, and the uniform came with him, to write down what I'd say.

McClaren stared at me for what seemed like a full minute. Then he sighed. "So tell me what kind of mess you got into now."

I recounted the trail that had led me to the house in Kennebunkport. I left out a few things that would have had them throw me in a cell along with the kidnappers. I gave him the van description and plate number of Steven's other captors. McClaren had the uniform go put out a BOLO, or "Be On the Lookout" for them, with a warning that they were armed and dangerous. They'd probably be picked up before long, unless they took to the backwoods.

It was hours before I could get cut loose from the questioning. I'd still have to go down to headquarters for a formal deposition, but they'd at least let me rest overnight. I might even have to testify eventually, unless the kidnappers took plea deals.

Allison was mighty unhappy at finding me hurt again, and even though I had a bullet in my leg, I was still feeling pretty pleased with myself. I had a pile of cash that nobody else knew about, one that might last me a while. Some of the bad guys were in a cell, and the rest would be caught soon. We didn't yet know if they could be tied to the artist's death, or Abernathy's, but with a minimum of kidnapping on the docket, they were looking at some serious prison time.

Most of all, I was happy for rescuing Steven. Whatever his flaws, he'd come through in the clinch. And he was Mrs. Harris's grandson, and I'd managed to restore him to the world. He still had to remain in Maine until everything got sorted out, but at least she could speak with him and make her peace. If he turned state's evidence against his captors, the state would likely let him off the forgery charges, saying it was all done under duress. And he'd inherit Mrs. Harris' estate, so he'd come out all right. All he seemed concerned about was Bosco. And I'd finished the job.

So it was with some satisfaction I called Saul Rabinowitz down in Miami. It was late afternoon, but I thought he'd still be there. His assistant put him through when I told her who I was.

"I found Steven," I said. "It's a long story, but he'd been kidnapped and forced to create art forgeries. He's with the police now, but you should be able to speak with him, set him up with an attorney, and get a connection between him and Mrs. Harris."

There was a silence on the other end.

"Hey, look," I said. "It's a mess, but I think he'll come out okay. The important thing is, I found him, and he's alive and well. You can tell Mrs. Harris he even saved me when I went to rescue him."

The voice was quiet, and I could hear some pain behind it. "I'm afraid Rita passed away in her sleep this morning."

I felt the Fates laughing at me once again.

Dale T. Phillips

CHAPTER 32

With my crutches and bandaged leg, I was once more in the hot seat at the police station, with McClaren presiding. Though I'd written out and signed a statement, I was being grilled, and it seemed like Fielding was out for my blood. Gordon, my red-headed attorney, sat beside me, in an attempt to keep me out of jail. He wrote things down from time to time. Some attorney was there on the other side of the table to represent the law, and he also kept scribbling things down.

Fielding was looking at me like I was from another planet. "Who the fuck are you, really?" He shook his head. "I do not understand why you did this, jumped into my case and blew it up like you did."

"You mean wrap up the criminal organization?" I was as mad and baffled as he was. I felt I'd actually done them a favor. "Just get one of those clowns to roll on the Holloways. I hear you got Bosco back, and even caught the two that killed Abernathy. And what about Perkins' bodyguard? He was working with Abernathy."

"I told you before, the Holloways don't give the orders to street goons like these. Not one claims to have even talked

179

to them. They gave orders to a guy that gave orders to someone else."

"So work your way up the ladder. It has to eventually lead to the Holloways. That's how Ollie got released, by giving up someone you want more."

"Yeah, sounds real easy, doesn't it? But we haven't caught the one above them yet. That was your friend with Abernathy in the parking lot. If we can't find him, we may not be able to make the connection. And now the damn Holloways are on guard."

"Yeah, but I got Steven free. Doesn't that count for anything?"

"It does," broke in McClaren, trying to calm the waters before things got physical. "He was producing good fakes in that house, a number of them. He told us they went for between fifty and eighty grand a pop."

"How'd he start doing fakes, anyway?"

"His boyfriend," said McClaren. "And the heroin habit, which was going on back when they were at that art retreat. Abernathy got him into the business."

"Does he know why they killed that other artist, the one they thought drowned?"

"The guy discovered what Steven was doing, said he was going to tell. Bosco dropped a dime on him to Abernathy, and the guy turns up dead. That scared the little shits, but Bosco started making trouble afterward. Steven said he felt guilty, so he was drinking and doing more drugs. That's what got them kicked out of the art place. Soon after, the ones who'd set this up realized they couldn't keep a lid on it, so they strapped Steven and Bosco down hard. Steven was kept in the forgery mill, and as long as he behaved himself and did good work, he got visits from Bosco, who bought his art supplies. He knew what to get, unlike the goons. And Bosco got all the heroin he wanted. After you scared him, they started babysitting Bosco like they did Steven."

"So their forgery ring is smashed and their soldiers are taken out. There's the house, the cars, the fake painting sales,

Abernathy. You're telling me none of it can be directly traced to the Holloways?"

Fielding shook his head. "Not a goddamned bit. I told you they were smart. That's a ding to their bottom line, sure, but it doesn't stop them. Which means it doesn't do me a fucking bit of good. All my leads are cut, and my case is blown, because they know we're watching. And that's on you."

I waved a hand. "So you don't give a rat's ass about anything else, like the bad money and drugs and crooks we got off the streets? Not to mention saving lives?"

Fielding glared at me. "Not my monkey, not my circus. All I know is, you fucked me. So I'm going to fuck you right back, hard, starting with charges for obstruction of justice. Lieutenant, would you do the honors and book this criminal?"

McClaren wouldn't meet my gaze. I was building up a head of steam. "Are you out of your goddamned mind? Arresting me, because you're pissed off that I did more harm to them in a few days than you've done in two years? And you're going to force the lieutenant here, who is a decent man, to do your dirty work for you? And you wonder why no one trusts you."

Gordon broke in. "This has all been a very entertaining farce, but I think it's time for it to end."

Fielding smiled. "You don't think I can make it stick?"

"Oh, I'm sure you could fuck yourself even harder than you have already," said Gordon. "But wouldn't you rather have a nice juicy lead to follow on the Holloways?"

"I told you, none of that shit will stick to them."

"This is something different," said Parker. "Something else my client discovered while he was so busy getting in your way, as you put it. It arrived yesterday, while he was getting shot, or he'd have turned it in by now."

"What is it?"

"A trail by which you can start tracing forged paintings back to the ones that brokered the deals. High-level dealers, one step below the Holloways, and probably acting on their orders. We have a list of buyers and the forged paintings they bought, and who they bought them from. Steven may have even painted them himself, and could identify them. It could lead you right to the Holloways' doorstep."

Fielding blinked and held out a hand. "Let me see it."

Parker cleared his throat. "In time. We'll trade it to you for full immunity for my client on all charges, state and federal, related to this or any other case you might drum up."

Fielding stared at him. The clock ticked off a few seconds, as he grappled with the balance of a good lead versus his desire to shut me in a cage. "That's evidence. I can subpoena that."

"Do you want full cooperation, or do you want to dig a deeper hole for yourself?"

The other attorney bent his head to whisper to Fielding. They had a quiet exchange for a minute, with some gesturing. Fielding's pinched face looked like he'd bitten into a lemon. "Fine. No charges for what he did, as long as this pans out. Now hand it over."

"I'd love to," said Parker. "But because you're such a treacherous dick, we'll need to see everything in writing. Immediately. A man's wife was attacked for this information, and she just passed away. So it's worth a lot. This offer is good until five o'clock today, at which time, if you have not replied in good faith, you will instead be served with papers detailing an extensive and expensive action for harassment, and that's just the start. Civil charges, at least, and maybe more, depending whether it can be proven how far you extended your reach. We'll see to it that this is the end of your career. We'll leave the Portland Police out of this, as long as they cooperate, which I feel they'll be happy to do. This is on you, and you ought to be ashamed of yourself. It's no wonder you haven't brought the Holloways to justice, if this is how you treat people."

I thought Fielding would blow up, his face was so red. He seemed to have trouble speaking. When he finally got the words out, his voice sounded like he was being choked. "You'll have your agreement."

"Then we've all won," said Parker, and stood. "And I believe that concludes our business, gentlemen. Good day."

Fielding stormed out of the room, followed by the other attorney.

McClaren looked at me and shook his head. "Nice save."

"Thanks."

"Before you go, it's interesting that you mentioned Ollie. One of our confidential informants, a biker, spotted him in Laconia, over in New Hampshire. So be on your guard."

I reached for my crutches. "It just never ends, does it?"

Dale T. Phillips

CHAPTER 33

I was still using a cane on the day Allison, J.C. and I were in the Portland Museum of Art, looking at the newly-installed Salvador Dali piece I had given them. Next to it on the wall was a small card that read *Donated In Memory of Marguerite Harris*. My name was not on the card, as it wasn't about me. I was also going to pay for a nice memorial for Cyrus' wife, so I felt like quite the benefactor.

"So beautiful," said Allison.

"One of the smartest and best things you've ever done," said J.C., nodding approval.

I shrugged. "We took it out of the crate and propped it against the coffee table all night. She drank wine, and we just looked at it. We realized that not only could we not take care of it, it deserved to be seen by everyone. Here, it will be seen."

J.C. was grinning. "And you didn't even sell it."

"Ah, but I do get a lifetime membership here," I said. "With invites to all their special events. And I can bring guests."

"I wondered why Allison stays with you. Now I know."

"Watch it," I said, and smiled. "I can have the security guard eject you." I called out. "Hey, Theo."

Theo came from where he'd been guarding the entryway.

"Meet the museum's newest security guard," I said. "One condition I insisted on when it was donated. I wanted this piece to be safe, and no one is going to mess with it when he's around."

"You just wanted to clear your guilty conscience," said Theo, flashing a smile.

J.C. gave me a raised eyebrow.

I shrugged. "Theo worked security for the movie. When it closed down, he lost his gig. I was responsible."

"How's the leg?" Theo looked down at my cane.

"Still aches. Doctor says another week, and I can stop using this damned cane, if I want."

"And you can start getting into trouble again," Theo nodded.

"He better not," said Allison. "He's going to go a whole month without having someone try to kill him, as a start."

"So that mess with the art forgery is settled?" J.C. eyed me.

"Mostly," I replied. "If they can't make a connection, though, looks like the Holloways will get away with it, since no one is rolling on them, at least yet. They never ordered the dirty stuff directly. They used other people, so the crimes can't be traced back to them. At least their criminal enterprise took a major hit."

"What about that house in Kennebunkport? Didn't they own that?"

"I'm sure they did, but the name on the deed was Abernathy."

"The gallery owner who was killed?" J.C. had been following the case.

"Yeah, he worked for the Holloways, funneling the forgeries through mutual connections. He's the one that got Steven involved, who wanted money to finance his boyfriend's heroin habit. All went well for them until another artist happened to see a painting that Steven was forging. He was going to blow the whistle, so Bosco told

Abernathy, and next thing the artist is found dead. The one Sonny's friend pulled up."

"I imagine that put a crimp in things," said J.C.

"You got that right," I said. "Steven knew it wasn't an accident, and was going to go to the cops, so they stashed him under guard in Kennebunkport, and said if he told, they'd kill him, after they tortured Bosco in front of him. Bosco had much less of a conscience, had his habit, and he was already an accessory to murder, so that kept him in line. He had to come once a week for cuddle time with Steven."

I took a breath, feeling for what had happened when I got into the scheme. "When I started poking around, Abernathy immediately set off the alarms. They were on Bosco alert, and came in fast when I spoke with him. Everyone got nervous, Abernathy most of all, since he was vulnerable. The Holloways must have thought he was more of a liability than an asset, and they had him taken out." I deliberately didn't mention the bag of cash I'd grabbed.

"But they didn't count on you," said J.C.

"I knew there was a house, and some link," I said. "The property deed holder matched a corporation in those files you gave me, but I didn't get it until after it all went down. I was glad Steven got out. He'll be quite a witness for the prosecution. The kidnappers have a lot of charges, and likely will be connected to one or both murders. And if Fielding can trace any of the forged art, maybe they can even nail the Holloways."

"So what happens now?" J.C. wanted more. Ever the reporter.

"Well, McClaren is pissed. There were so many laws broken in so many areas, it's going to be one hell of a bureaucratic nightmare. His world is going to be a mountain of paperwork, hundreds of phone calls, and deals with prosecutors, judges and other departments over search warrants and coordinating all charges. Hope he didn't have a vacation planned for a while."

"What happens to Steven?"

"He's in protective custody, and was happy to tell them about his forced captivity. He'll turn state's evidence. Then he gets to inherit Mrs. Harris' estate. His friend Bosco was sent to rehab for his heroin habit, the condition of him staying out of jail. I don't know if he'll do okay or not, and I don't much care. He caused another person's death to save his own skin, and he let others take the fall while he pretended to live the life of an artist."

Allison shook her head. "All that from a deathbed promise to find someone. He's got a talent for turning over rocks and finding the worst stuff."

"Let's forget about all that," I said. "And focus on the good. Like this picture."

As the afternoon sun slanted in to highlight the painting, I was reminded of Mrs. Harris. Because of her, people in a place far away from where she had spent her last years could enjoy a moment of sublime beauty. Something of her would live on and touch the lives of others. Even if the moment was ephemeral, a life would be better by being exposed to that truth and beauty, something Keats had written about. Perhaps all we ever had was fleeting moments, and that was why we should enjoy them all the more.

CHAPTER 34

With things settled, I now had free time on my hands. I asked Allison if she wanted to go see the show at a gallery. I had reasons other than art.

The Holloways had played it smart so far in their career, and kept enough distance between themselves and their criminal endeavors. Nothing could be proven against them in court yet, confirming that if you're smart or lucky enough, you can indeed get away with murder. They reminded me of some of the mobsters I'd known, the clever ones who never got down in the trenches anymore, just had guys doing their dirty work, and presented themselves as pillars of the community.

So I wanted to put them on notice that I was watching, that the hounds of hell were on their trail. Guys who dealt with the darkness didn't like being watched. Maybe they'd react eventually, make a mistake. I wanted them nervous, putting it into their shared thoughts that one error, one slip-up from now on, and it could all come crashing down around them.

I figured playing watchdog was a way of paying off my karmic debt of my earlier years. Though I'd been around mob guys, I hadn't done anything illegal in those days. I was strictly contract bodyguard help, and they never talked that kind of business around me. When we did chat, it was mostly about women, money, sports, and gambling, and who was tougher, that kind of crap. But my conscience pricked me from time to time. If I hadn't hung out with crooks, I wouldn't have landed in prison, wrongly or not. Or maybe I would have anyway, maybe that was my fate.

But all Allison had to know was that we were going to a gallery opening to see and talk with artists. She didn't seem bitter about being exposed to something she'd given up as a career, and might even take up painting again. I was in favor of anything that made her happier.

So we ate a great meal at an Italian place with music, candles, the whole bit. She drank wine and laughed, and I just smiled and smiled. I'd given up a painting worth a fortune, but had found another little windfall, and so had enough money to last me until I figured out what I wanted to do next.

We drove down to Ogunquit on a fine night, and strolled along to the gallery, arm-in-arm. All was right with the world. Maybe I'd failed to enact Mrs. Harris' dying wish, but I'd probably saved the kid's life, after all, even if he was in trouble for the time being. They couldn't have kept up that scam forever, and guys who do dirty deals don't like inconvenient witnesses hanging around. As it was, he'd come out all right, and he'd have one more chance.

The gallery was buzzing with excited voices from little knots of people doing more talking than looking at the art. Allison got a glass of wine, and we began our rounds. I looked for the Holloways, and they were at opposite ends of the room, working the crowd. There were a number of large sculptures around the place, so maybe they hadn't noticed me yet, but I couldn't be sure. They'd probably be polite in this crowd. But their career was built on murder and theft, and I wondered if the people here knew or cared about any of that.

I looked at the rich patrons and successful gallery, and couldn't help thinking about my broken dreams of having a place where people could come and experience another world. Sure, a karate dojo was different from an art gallery, but both had a purpose, and were built on providing something for people to share. My dream had ended because of some psycho with a couple of cans of gasoline and a taste for revenge. I forced myself to push these thoughts aside.

We took our time enjoying the new pieces on display. There was one set Allison was particularly fond of, a series of portraits in oil. I'd have liked to get one for her, but with a five-figure price tag, I thought it was a bit much. She got another glass of wine, and we moved on to the next set of pictures.

I sensed the wrong kind of movement at the door, and looked up. Two men had entered, wearing long coats, ball caps, and dark sunglasses. One had a beard, and the other wore a hooded sweatshirt, his face obscured. They both carried shotguns.

There was a collective gasping and a scream, and the crowd parted as they came forward.

"We just want money, watches, and jewels," called out the bearded one. "But if anyone does something stupid, people are going to die. Do what we say and no one gets hurt. Real slow now, everybody lie down."

A room full of people held hostage by two men. There wasn't much else to do but comply. If I tried anything, people would get hurt. With fear so thick in the air you could smell it, the guests got down as best they could, while the second man snapped out a large black garbage bag, still holding the shotgun with the other hand.

Beard-man spoke again. "The bag's going around. I want to see all the wallets and every bit of shiny shit you're wearing go in there. Rings, everything. Anybody decides to get cute, or hold out, they're gonna have a real bad night."

The bag was passed around, and people placed their valuables in it. I had my head tilted to watch the two intruders, but hadn't moved otherwise.

The hooded guy turned toward me. "What did you say?" Something was wrong. He should have been more interested to see that every person made a complete donation.

An Arctic wave of cold washed over me. I hadn't made a peep, but I knew the raspy voice in an instant as that of Ollie Southern, the psycho who had burned my dojo. I also knew I was about to die. It was a goddamn setup, an execution made to look like a robbery.

"Looks like we got us a hero," Ollie said over his shoulder.

I'd braced a foot against the floor, and pushed off in a roll as the shotgun blasted the world apart. Steel pellets of buckshot tore into my arm as I flipped myself behind a sculpture made of concrete. The second explosion struck the piece, and there was nowhere to go for me. All he had to do was take a few steps, and I had nowhere to hide, no way to stop from being slaughtered. Sheltered for a second behind a chunk of blasted concrete, I removed a shoe. It was nothing, but I'd throw it at him anyway, one last stupid act of defiance, my last in the world. Angry and violent to the end, meeting a fate on a path that was set long ago.

But there were more explosions, sharp cracks instead of the booming shotguns. I glanced to my left, and there was one of the Holloways with a small handgun, firing from where he lay. Two shotguns thundered again, and there were no more shots, just screams. Lots of them.

I poked my head around the far side of the sculpture. Ollie was on the floor. The bearded guy was down, too. I jumped to my feet, the first person up, and hurried to Ollie's body. The blown-out back of his head was a bloody mess. Holloway had shot well. I picked up the shotgun, training it on the other fallen robber, just in case. He was on his back, arms wide, with three spreading spots of red on his chest. His eyes were open in a look of surprise, the light inside them fading fast. I took his shotgun away, and looked around at the people now struggling to their feet. There were sobs now, male and female.

I ran to Allison and knelt by her, setting down the shotguns. She had a red line across her forehead, probably from a pellet that had ricocheted. Blood ran into her eyes. I whipped out my handkerchief and pressed it against the wound. I looked for any other marks, but that was all that was visible. "Are you okay?"

She buried her head in my chest, great heaving gusts wracking her body. I held her and tried to say soothing things.

One of the Holloways was kneeling over a body. His twin. With both of them firing, they'd brought down the killers, but beard-man had responded with his own kill. Other people were wailing, and I knew some others must have got hit.

With blood dripping from my arm, and injured folk all around, I held everything I loved in the world and rocked Allison, counting us fortunate to be alive. Ollie's face was turned to me, and on it shone a certain slant of light, a peculiar shaft of illumination that made his features look almost angelic in death.

THE END

Dale T. Phillips

LIKE MORE ZACK TAYLOR?

Sign up for my newsletter to get discounts on upcoming titles
OR- Get a free ebook or audio book
At http://www.daletphillips.com

A SHARP MEDICINE

Zack Taylor's life is once again in shambles. Having narrowly escaped death, guilty over the pain he's caused a loved one, and hounded by the press, he's living as a recluse. When asked to look into the disappearance of a young reporter, Zack uncovers corruption and evil in a world of politics, passion, and power.

Read on for the first chapter of *A Sharp Medicine*, **the fifth book of the Zack Taylor series.**

CHAPTER 1

The woman I loved was in rehab, and it was my fault. Some wouldn't blame me, because after all, who would think an art gallery opening would erupt in gunfire? But I knew I'd been wrong to take her there, wrong to get her involved at all, because of the violence that was never far from me. It was the Law of Unintended Consequences, as my friend J.C. Reed had explained to me.

Because we'd almost died there, Allison had been affected far more than I understood at first. To stop the nightmares and flashbacks, she began drinking more and

195

more. It soon took her over the edge, as it once had done with me. She started missing work, an especially bad thing for an ER nurse, and eventually they let her go. Which of course, only made her drinking worse.

J.C. and I had done an impromptu intervention, and essentially kidnapped her and got her compliant enough to sign herself into a private specialty clinic on the ocean, a little ways north of Portland. She seemed to be doing better there, but of course, most things were better than blackout drinking. I knew from first-hand experience. A now-deceased friend had done something similar for me years ago, except the rehab facility was the Maine wilderness. It's tough to find a drink when you're a hundred miles from the nearest bar or liquor store.

There was good counseling in the place we'd taken her, which helped with her trauma from the incident, and she was slowly drying out. It was expensive, but since it was my fault, I was paying for the whole thing with a stash of illicit money I'd got in my last adventure. But it was disappearing fast.

Another problem was the unwanted publicity, fanned to tabloid frenzy by Mason Carter, a scandal-sheet hack with a nasty streak. Though it was supposed to be my execution masquerading as a robbery, he portrayed it as a gangland slaying. He'd dubbed it "The Shooting Gallery," and the phrase had been picked up by other papers eager for sensational headlines. Carter had a grudge against me, and trotted out all his old insinuations about my dark dealings, most of which existed only in his head. Which was ironic, because the truth about what I did was much darker than the crap he peddled. While I wasn't officially in hiding, I was trying to keep a low profile until it all blew over. Maine wasn't used to big gun battles in public places, so this was major news, but without further fuel, the fire would die out after a while.

J.C. had arranged for me to stay at the house of a friend of his who was off in China somewhere. So the reporters couldn't find me, and all they could do was publish grainy pictures with titles like *"Where is the Mystery Man?"* I'd taken to wearing Red Sox caps and dark sunglasses, feeling like a movie star stalked by paparazzi. I now understood what they felt like, afraid of being recognized and hounded every time they left the sanctity of their abode.

But I was getting restless just living in the shadows. I'd done that for a good part of my life, and had been trying to change before all this happened. I needed something to do, I couldn't just sit inside and read all day. I couldn't just up and leave, because we visited Allison twice a week. It had taken some long talks with the doctors before they'd let me see her, but they finally agreed that my presence wouldn't make her worse.

When J.C. said he wanted me to meet someone, my pulse quickened. It sounded like my adopted line of work, which was helping people in trouble. My business card read *Security Consultant*, which covered a pretty broad range of activities. My checkered past disqualified me for most other professions, but I did have a knack for turning over rocks to find out the secrets beneath.

We met at a restaurant in Lewiston that billed itself as Polynesian, which puzzled me, because J.C. loved good food and drink, knew all the best places for dining, and there were dozens of them around us that didn't require a 30-minute drive.

J.C. made introductions. "Zack Taylor, meet Bob LaFollette,"

Bob topped out at five-six, over four inches shorter than me, thin, late fifties. He wore glasses and had a worried air. His handshake was firm, though. No calluses, so he didn't work with his hands.

I noted that J.C. didn't have his usual tumbler of scotch before him, and they'd been seated when I arrived. For a guy that looked a lot like Hemingway and sometimes drank to match, this was quite the anomaly. And having J.C. call me for a favor was odd, too, as he blamed me for Allison's problem.

I looked around at the décor. "What's with this place? Don't tell me they have a particular dish you can't get anywhere else."

J.C. gave me a look like I was an idiot.

The light dawned. "Ah. No one you'd know would ever come here, so neither you nor I would be recognized. And I'm guessing the food is probably as bad as the ambiance."

"We're not eating here. I told them to just leave us be," J.C. nodded. "Bob here runs a weekly newspaper on the coast."

The anger ran ahead of my thought processes. I'd been hounded by so many people from the papers, I lumped them as a group and hated them all. Except for J.C. himself, who worked for the *Maine Times*.

"What are you doing? What were you thinking?" I was about to get a good head of steam, but J.C. cut me off.

"This isn't about you. He's not here to detail your messes."

"Then what?"

"One of my reporters is missing," Bob's voice was quiet, and the lines on his face seemed to deepen. "A young woman."

I closed my mouth, which had once more been about to run without my brain connected. I took a deep breath and pushed the anger back down so I could think. "Okay. Tell me."

Bob pushed over a photograph. "Georgette Chapelle. Twenty-six. Worked for me for almost a year. Did good work, wanted more, wanted bigger. Always looking for the story that would be her break, the next step up."

I frowned. "She looks familiar. Was she on TV or something?"

"No. You might have seen her for one of your court cases."

198

"Yeah, that's it. She tagged me outside the courthouse once, tried asking me a couple of questions, and I played stupid."

"Easy for you," J.C. piped in. I shot him a dirty look.

Bob nodded. "She'd read some of that Mason Carter crap, wanted to know if there was anything to it. So she went to Portland, took a look around. Decided there was too much competition. Every reporter in the state was there. She liked the stories no one else was doing."

"How long has she been gone?"

"Don't know for sure. At least a few days."

"Was she working some new story?"

"Yeah, but she wouldn't say what. She should have checked in by now, and I'm getting worried."

"You think whatever she was working on might have got her into trouble?"

"I do. The scary stories have the most appeal. She might have got in over her head."

"Have you talked to the police?"

Bob took off his glasses and polished them with a napkin before answering. "No. She might have gone undercover, and if her picture is splashed all over the news, it could put her in more trouble."

"So you don't want to raise the alarm in a general sense, just in case."

Bob nodded. "But I need to know she's okay. I didn't have a clue how to go about getting in touch with her, so I called J.C."

I frowned. "What about her family?"

"Gone. No brothers or sisters, her mom and dad passed away. She's had to make it on her own through some tough times, and that shaped her as a reporter. Spunky kid. Likeable. She wanted to use this photo for her own byline."

I looked closer at the photo he handed me. Nice young woman, smiling, but a small crease in her brow that showed she had a serious streak. Shortish hair, brown, looked like she could have still been in college.

"Can I keep this? I may need to show it around."

"Sure. Here's her address, but when I've gone by, there's no one there, and she doesn't answer messages. I'm at my wit's end."

"Okay. I'll see what I can do."

Bob ducked his head as if embarrassed. "About paying you. I can get a little now, and—"

I waved my hand. "Don't worry about it."

"But—"

J.C. put a light hand on Bob's arm. "It's covered, Bob. And despite what I say about this guy, if anyone can find her, it's him."

I wished I'd been as sure as J.C.

AFTERWORD

A Certain Slant of Light is the fourth in the series about Zack Taylor, a man with many problems. He struggles to do better, but the deeds of his past weigh him down. When he tries to help others, he finds that doing good is a complicated matter, and unintended consequences force life-changing alterations.

He is more acquainted with death than most people are, and so responds to the poetry of Emily Dickinson, whose frank discussions of the subject are cause for understanding.

There is much to think about for those who wish to peel back the layers. If not, just enjoy a cracking action yarn.

Should you be startled at certain anachronisms, such as the concept of pay phones, it's because this book is set in the 1990's.

But this is a work of fiction, and any resemblance to actual persons, living or dead, is purely coincidental.

Dale T. Phillips

ABOUT THE AUTHOR

A lifelong student of mysteries, Maine, and the martial arts, Dale T. Phillips has combined all of these into *A Certain Slant of Light*. His travels and background allow him to paint a compelling picture of Zack Taylor, a man with a mission, but one at odds with himself and his new environment.

A longtime follower of mystery fiction, the author has crafted a hero in the mold of Travis McGee, Doc Ford, and John Cain, a moral man at heart who finds himself faced with difficult choices in a dangerous world. But Maine is different from the mean, big-city streets of New York, Boston, or L.A., and Zack must learn quickly if he is to survive.

Dale studied writing with Stephen King, and has published novels, over 50 short stories, collections, as well as poetry, articles, and non-fiction. He has appeared on stage, television, and in an independent feature film, *Throg*. He has also appeared on two nationally televised quiz shows, *Jeopardy* and *Think Twice*. He co-wrote and acted in *The Nine*, a short political satire film. He has traveled to all 50 states, Mexico, Canada, and through Europe.

Connect Online:
Website: http://www.daletphillips.com
Blog: http://daletphillips@blogspot.com
Twitter: DalePhillips2

Try these other works by Dale T. Phillips

Shadow of the Wendigo (Supernatural Thriller)

Dale T. Phillips

The Zack Taylor Mystery Series
A Memory of Grief
A Fall From Grace
A Shadow on the Wall

Story Collections
Fables and Fantasies (Fantasy)
Crooked Paths (Mystery/Crime)
More Crooked Paths (Mystery/Crime)
Strange Tales (Magic Realism, Paranormal)
Apocalypse Tango (Science Fiction)
Halls of Horror (Horror)
Jumble Sale (Mixed Genres)
The Big Book of Genre Stories (Different Genres)

Non-fiction Career Help
How to Improve Your Interviewing Skills

With Other Authors
Insanity Tales
Insanity Tales II: The Sense of Fear
Rogue Wave: Best New England Crime Stories 2015
Red Dawn: Best New England Crime Stories 2016

Sign up for my newsletter to get special offers
http://www.daletphillips.com